DOGS, CARS, AND OLD MEN

Ten Short Stories

Richard Bustetter

Text Copyright © 2017 Richard Bustetter
All Rights Reserved

ISBN: 1537262599
ISBN 13: 9781537262598
Library of Congress Control Number: 2016915106
CreateSpace Independent Publishing Platform
North Charleston, South Carolina

DEDICATION

This collection of short stories is dedicated to my professors at University of Portland who inspired me to develop nascent ideas into completed projects. Most importantly these stories are dedicated to the people I met who inspired the characters in these stories. Great thanks go out to people with such individuality.

Kindle books by Richard Bustetter:

Dogs, Cars, and Old men: Ten short stories by Richard Bustetter

TABLE OF CONTENTS

A Saint Bernard	1
Brother Louis	53
Butol Oblonski	70
Cadillac Cab	94
Chuli and Yo-Yo	102
Curly	106
Henry and Silver	128
Katie's Story	146
Motor Terry	175
The Old Man	182
About the Author	187

A SAINT BERNARD

My house never used to be quite like this. Well I guess it was. Then it wasn't. Now it is again. I'm older now, almost fifteen. I have a girlfriend and the house is almost like it was when I first moved in with my grandpa Bertrand Brown. I did get some different furniture. My grandpa took me into his lemon yellow house with the green shutters next to the windows when I was a little kid. His was the only yellow house in the area. Over the years, because grandpa told me, I understood some of the things people expect of their neighbors when it comes to how a house is supposed to look. How the lawn is kept, tree maintenance stuff, the color of your house, all kinds of things. When my grandpa and grandma first moved into their house they had to do quite a bit of fixing things up. When they painted it some of the neighbors didn't like the lemon yellow color, but they were glad my grandparents had improved the place so much.

Their house, now my house, is on Ninth Avenue in central Yakima, Washington, two blocks south of what was originally named St. Elizabeth's hospital which was run by the Sisters of

Providence. Over the years the hospital changed its name a few times due to new ownership. A couple of blocks away there was a fire training station for the city firemen that occupied about half of the block on seventh avenue between Walnut and Chestnut streets. When my grandparents first moved to their house an electric train still ran through town on Pine Street, a couple blocks south of their house. The Yakima Valley Transit had a yellow electric locomotive that pulled full size box cars back and forth from west of Yakima, as well as out toward Selah, a small town north of Yakima. They moved tons and tons of fruit from lots of orchards, apples, pears, peaches, plums, cherries, with multiple varieties of those fruits. The train doesn't operate anymore, but the city uses the old tracks that run up Sixth Avenue on their way out to Selah to operate a seasonal trolley car. The train tracks are still right in the middle of Pine Street where they run from the Trolley station between Fifth and Third Avenues, all the way to Eleventh Avenue. Where they have been decommissioned. Which means the tracks end. I've seen the Trolley running, but I've never ridden on it. I grew up hearing about or seeing all kinds of things that happened in our area. Which I guess are all the same kinds of things that take place in neighborhoods wherever people live.

Now when I walk into my house the place smells good, clean and natural, kind of outdoorsy. Everything is clean and tidy. Pictures are dusted, hanging straight. Even the old painting of Maximus, my grandpa's St. Bernard is hanging straight. The house is orderly now. Things are picked up and put away. It's like when my grandpa was still alive living here with me and taking care of me by himself.

Those years when I lived here with only my grandpa were great. But, one day my grandpa died. Then my dad moved in. When my dad first moved in with me things were okay. Then it got messy, dirty. But, within a short time, days really, it was a disaster. It stayed a disaster until my dad died. Then I had to clean it up again. But it wasn't only the house I cleaned up.

I inherited my grandpa's house. He left it to me so I would have a place to live. He must have figured if I owned the place I would always have a place to live. Grandpa was real good to me. I'm so grateful he made it that way.

I got my grandpa's house when he died instead of anybody else when I was barely fourteen. I wasn't old enough to get a job so I could live on my own. Having a place to live kept me safe off the street. I wouldn't have had anywhere to go if grandpa hadn't given me his paid-off house. He also set it up so the taxes and insurance got paid. I didn't know about any of that stuff until later. I know he told me about those things, but at the time I didn't really understand about all that kind of stuff. I didn't have to. Grandpa set it up all automatic-like so I didn't have to worry about where I lived.

Grandpa told me I would have to take care of Maximus too. That is if something happened to him. Which was fine to me. I didn't want anything bad to happen to my grandpa. Of course I didn't understand all the arrangements he made for me, not completely anyway. That was okay though because grandpa had some good friends that helped him figure out how to make things all okay for me.

In the first place I was living with my grandpa because otherwise I wouldn't have had anywhere to live. Which happened like this. I lived with my grandpa because my dad and mom didn't take care of me. Of course I didn't know about why my own parents didn't take care of me when I was little. I don't even know exactly how old I was when I started living with grandpa. I couldn't have been very old, two, or three, at the most.

I found out later what my parents were into, which was drugging and drinking and whatever went along with that. They never came to visit. Well, mostly never. My dad came by once in a while, like about every few years or so, only to have grandpa shoo him away before he could spend the night. Sometime when I was about six or seven grandpa told me my mom died. He said she died in some kind of accident. He was trying to be nice to me, so at the time she died he didn't tell me what really happened to her. What grandpa told me later, when I was a little older, was that her so-called accident involved buying some hot heroin that may have had a little heroin in it, but was mostly something else. Anyway she died. She was about twenty-two or three. No one knew for sure.

Grandpa told me that my mom and dad were together and then not together, off again on again with each other. My mom did lots of stuff to stay high. My dad mostly drank. I'm pretty sure that's about all he did. What they did for money and where they lived wasn't what I knew about while I grew up at grandpa's place. Once I moved in, was moved in, got dropped off, or whatever or however I came to be with grandpa, I had a normal life.

Except for being raised by my Dad's dad instead of my own parents I had it good. Grandpa took exceptional care of me. I ate really well all the time. He started me in school. Got me involved in sports, little league baseball, football and basketball at school. He even got me started playing the guitar; because, that's what he did. He played the guitar a lot. He was real good. He had made a living playing the guitar. He used to play in clubs and bands and had made enough money so that he didn't have to play for other people anymore. I found out later that he had stopped going out at night to play music as much as he used to after I showed up as a permanent fixture in his house.

Later on I realized the biggest reason he stayed home more was that my grandma had died from cancer shortly before I was moved in with grandpa. I never got to know my grandma. She was the real reason grandpa retired from professional guitar gigs. He stayed home to take care of her. After she died he played guitar in some local clubs a little, although not nearly as much as he used to. It wasn't more than a month after she died that I started living with grandpa. I was so little I didn't know the details at the time. Which was okay to me then and now.

Dogs, Cars, and Old Men

    I lived a great life with my grandpa. I know what it means to be loved by someone. By the time I was fourteen I had learned a lot. Had grown up a lot. Had gotten pretty big for a fourteen-year-old. I got to be pretty tall. Six feet three inches. I weighed one hundred and ninety pounds. With grandpa cooking for me I got big. I wasn't fat though. Grandpa had gotten me into the different school sports where I learned to lift weights. I had a lot of interest from the school coaches in me for playing various sports. Mostly football since I was big and strong.

    I had all these things going for me. From about the time I turned thirteen once a month or so grandpa would ask me. Mr. Daryl Brown, "Someday I'm going to be gone and you're going to have to take care of yourself. Can you do that?"

    I would always tell him, "Sure grandpa, you taught me how to be a man. I'll be able to take care of myself." Knowing in my heart I was scared to death he would die. I didn't want to lose him. I didn't want to lose the man who loved me enough to take me in when I was a baby kid so he could raise me up to be who I am today. I wanted him to know I loved him by telling him he had done a great job. I was grateful beyond words I knew at the time. Then when I turned fourteen he started asking me the same thing about once a week. I would always give him the same answer changing the words a little. I'd say, "Of course I'll be able to take care of myself." I loved my grandpa so much. He was always honest with me, except for things he thought I didn't need to know about my mom and dad. He told me lots of things about my parents. Mostly good things he wanted me to remember. Over the years I lived with him he did tell me about them being involved with drugs and alcohol. He didn't give me lots of details. Mostly he told me that they were incapable of taking care of me due to their own problems. We had some great talks.

    Then it happened. School had been going for a couple of months. The days were getting shorter. I came home from school one afternoon to find grandpa Bertrand slumped over his favorite old D-35 Martin guitar. His right arm hung down across the strings as his right hand pointed toward the floor. His head drooped down with his chin resting on the shoulder of the guitar. His left arm rested on the seat cushion of the burgundy leather sofa. I had never seen a dead person before. I kept looking to see if he was really dead. I squatted down on the floor in front of him. He looked like he could have been sleeping. That Martin guitar he had played for so many years kept him from collapsing onto the floor.

I put my left hand behind his head. With my left elbow steadying his right shoulder I put my right hand up under his left arm. I gently pushed him back against the back of the sofa. I picked up his right arm so I could take his guitar from him. While he sat against the sofa with his arms at his sides I took his guitar from him so I could set it on the stand he always used. Then I leaned into him to give him a tight hug. I nestled my right cheek up against the right side of his neck. His skin was smooth, clean shaven, cooler than usual. He smelled like Old Spice. Then I began to cry. Not a little. I cried like no human had ever cried before. My tears ran down my face like hot little rivers. I blubbered like a baby. "Oh grandpa," I said as I hugged him so close to me I thought I might be able to bring him back to life.

After a while I let him go. That was the last time I hugged him. He wanted me to be a man. So I decided to be the man he taught me to be. I rearranged him against the sofa so he looked comfortable.

Then I went over to his desk where he kept his important things. I found the envelope he told me about inside the top drawer for what to do in case he died. It wasn't big. Only a letter size white envelope with the words: "Instructions for Daryl", written in his clear penmanship with a fine-tipped black permanent marker. Inside I found the instructions he left for me. It was a list of three phone numbers. The first one was his pastor. The second one was for the funeral home. The third was to his lawyer.

I called them all in that order. They took care of everything just like grandpa instructed them to do some years ago when he had planned his funeral arrangements. There wasn't much for me to do except what other people said for me to do. I met some of my grandpa's friends at the funeral. They were all real nice to me. As far as I knew I was the only person related to him that went to his funeral.

Around the time after the funeral I spent a few days away from school. Then I went back as usual. When I came home from school, or anywhere else for that matter, Maximus was always happy to see me. His big sloppy jaw full of saliva wasn't my favorite thing about him so I wasn't as affectionate with him as grandpa had been. I wanted him to sleep outside to keep me safe, which he did. There were also times I wanted him in at night for company. He could be very intimidating to people he didn't know. Except for grandpa he was one of my best friends.

My grandpa hadn't been gone a week when I came home from school one day to find Maximus tied with a chain attached to a metal post stuck in the grass in front of the house. It was a pretty short chain. It had been tied in a kind of tangle into his collar and looked like it was uncomfortable to him. He really couldn't go more than about four feet in any direction. I was puzzled about what was going on. Until I heard some noise in the back of the house. I was kind of scared what it might be. I let Maximus off the chain. He led me around to the back porch of the house. He was barking and making a fuss. The kind of bark he could do that had made more than one of my grandpa's friends shit their pants when they surprised Maximus inside the house. When I caught up to him I could see he was barking at a man on the back porch. With me there his bark had settled down a little. It wasn't quite the "I'm going to scare-the-shit-out-of-you-bark," he had been doing earlier. As soon as I looked at the man he said to me.

"Well, hello son," he said.

I was taken aback. There was a man sitting on my back porch. He was drinking something out of a bottle that was wrapped in a brown paper bag. The top of the bag was all wrinkled up from where he was holding it. I could smell the odor of liquor floating in the air.

"Shut up dog," the man shouted.

"Dad?" I asked. "Quiet down Maximus," I said as I rubbed the dog on the head.

"Of course it's me Daryl. Bertrand Brown the second in the flesh. Who else would claim you? Why don't you put that dog back on its leash? He makes way too much noise."

I patted Maximus on the head some more. He stopped barking.

"So my old man finally kicked the bucket huh?" he asked.

I stood still silently looking at my disheveled dad. I wondered if it was actually him. The longer I stood there the more I kept smelling that inside bottom of a dumpster kind of odor. Like all kinds of things mixed up and left to rot for a while. The liquor smell that was like a small cloud hovering around him made the dumpster smell even stronger.

"I know you're glad I'm back. I came here to be with my boy, you know."

"Grandpa died about a week ago. I didn't see you at the funeral. You look different," I said.

"I was real busy that day," he said.

Then I stood there looking at him for a while. He was messy. He smelled bad. His shoes looked like the newest part of his clothes. This is my dad I kept asking and telling myself all at the same time. I was confused though. Why was he here now I wondered?

"Nice shoes," I said.

"Yeah, I got this pair about two weeks ago. A friend of mine left them for me. He died, about two weeks ago."

"Oh," I said.

"Ready to go in now?" he said.

"Uh, yeah, I guess so," I said.

I watched him get up off the wooden steps of the back porch. He seemed like he was sore or stiff or something. He was holding his hand over his big lower stomach area.

Maximus and I followed him around to the front of the house. Maximus waited on the lawn while my dad and I went up onto the front porch. It took my dad a little effort to get himself up the three steps that led onto the small porch which served as the landing entrance for the front door of the house, but he made it. He stood between the outer screen door and the front door so I would let him in. I got pretty close to him as he stood there looking up into my face. Which was when I realized I was nearly half a foot taller than him. I had to ask him to move back so I could unlock the dead bolt of the main door so we could get in the house. He smiled a rotten tooth grin at me. I barely recognized him from the last time he came around. His breath had a kind of sweet alcohol sugary kind of smell to it. Not at all what I expected. Whatever it was, his breath wasn't right. Maybe he had some kind of sickness.

I unlocked the door with my key then let it swing open. Squeezing himself between me and the front door he went into the house in front of me. He went toward the middle of the front room as I took my key out of the lock to put it back in my pocket.

"You stay out for now Maximus," I said to my dog who had come up onto the porch to follow me in. I went in through the front door, closed it, and then listened to the wooden screen door bang itself shut. My dad went right up to the pictures hanging on the walls. He looked like he was squinting at them. I figured he probably needed glasses.

I set my things down on the arm of the couch then sank into the cushion on the end opposite the spot where my grandpa had died. I watched this sick appearing man wander slowly around the room. He was looking closely at things. It was as if he was looking for something in particular. He touched the top of my grandpa's D-35 guitar that I left in its stand near the end of the couch. I could see him smile a little when he gently rubbed the tuning head for the D string between his thumb and forefinger. He looked like he might have been reminiscing. He rubbed his chin with his right hand. Then he wandered around the room looking at photos and pictures on the walls.

"I do look a little different don't I?" he said.

I wondered what he was really thinking. "So you think you're really my dad?"

"Quit it kid. You know I'm your dad. It's me in all these old pictures. It's like this kid. Who else in the world would claim you?"

"Grandpa Bertrand," I said.

"I'm just a little down on my luck. I need a little cleaning up. You'll see I look exactly like I did in these pictures," he said.

"Except for the teeth," I said.

"What did you say to me?" he said angry like.

"Your teeth don't look like they used to," I said. Admitting to myself that this guy saying he was really my dad wasn't easy for me. I knew it was him. I just didn't want someone who looked, acted and talked like this guy to be my dad. Even though the minute I saw him I knew in my heart it was my dad. He had come home to see me.

He rolled his eyes at me, then said, "So, what's for dinner?" he asked.

"You're staying for dinner?" I asked.

"I'm going to be staying with you all the time now son," he said. "You heard me didn't you? I'm home for good to be with my son."

"You are?" I asked.

"Well sure. Now that your gramps is gone you oughtn't to be rattling around in this place all alone," he said.

"I don't think grandpa would like that very much," I said.

"Now that he's gone I'm sure he wouldn't want a young boy like you living here all by yourself. Don't forget he's gone. And don't you forget I'm your father."

"You may be my father, but grandpa set it up through his attorney that I'm emancipated. I'm my own legal man right now."

"What the hell are you talking about? You're just a kid."

"I'm fourteen. In the eyes of the law I'm a free man. It's called emancipation. I'm considered an adult. When grandpa died I got emancipated."

"You're a kid."

"That's what you say. The thing is since grandpa took care of me and my parents were not taking care of me he got it fixed so that when he died I would be my own man. As far as the whole world is concerned I'm a man."

"Bullshit"

"It's the truth. Not you or anybody else can change it."

He looked at me real mad like and said, "You think you're a man? Let me tell you something kid. You're not a man. You're a punk kid who's going to do what I tell you. I'm your old man. Your gramps is dead and gone. He can't help you now. I'm living in this house. This is my home. Whether you like it or not I'm living here. So shut up about any other crap you got stuck in your head."

Maximus was on the front porch barking through the screen door during my dad's speech to me. I knew something was wrong with my dad moving in with me. But, after all he was still my dad.

"Shut up that damn dog if you can why don't you?" he said.

It didn't matter much to me what he said. For some reason I had no fear whatsoever of my dad. Nothing he said scared me. I slowly got up from the couch. I could see he watched closely as me, his hundred-ninety-pound, six-foot-three, fourteen-year-old son stood all the way up. My dad stood about three feet away from me with his left shoulder facing me, he had his head cocked to his left side. We both knew I was bigger, taller and a lot stronger than he was. He was blowing a lot of hot air by trying to intimidate me. I walked over to the front door to go outside. I closed the main door behind me, gently kept the screen from slamming then I sat down on the top porch step next to Maximus. He was a slobber mess as usual as he nuzzled up to me. I put my right elbow on his back so I could scratch the top of his head and behind his ears. That was what grandpa told me Maximus liked so I always did it. He usually calmed down when I petted him like that.

"What are we going to do Maximus?" I said.

I got that feeling like someone was watching me. I looked over my left shoulder at the living room window to see my dad peering out at me and Maximus. I gave him a little wave. I didn't smile at him. Then I went back to petting Maximus.

I sat there for a while looking around at what was happening on my street. Cars went past. Kids were walking home from school. It was pretty quiet for a school day. A few people waved at me. I waved back. Maximus barked a couple of times to say hello when I waved at someone. A couple of neighbor kids called my name when they as usual said hi to Max. I always called him Maximus, but some people insisted on calling him Max. I always thought Maximus was a more dignified name. He was like grandpa. They were both old and dignified.

I wanted to be like my grandpa. I wanted to be dignified. I sat there until the street lights started coming on, thinking of what to do. I decided that the dignified thing to do would be to let my dad stay in my house, with me. I didn't have to. At least I didn't think I had to. But I couldn't help thinking how my grandpa took me in when I didn't have anybody or anyplace to turn to. It seemed to me like that was what I should do for my dad.

I went back in the house. I left Maximus outside. I could hear my Dad rooting around in the kitchen so I went in to see what he was doing. His head was illuminated by the light coming from inside the refrigerator because he hadn't turned on the overhead kitchen light. I quietly walked up to the kitchen entry to flip on the kitchen ceiling light. When the light went on my dad jumped back from the fridge. He looked around the room, then took a couple of deep breaths.

"Don't scare me like that boy!" he said. "I could have had another heart attack."

"You've had a heart attack?" I said. Then fleeting thoughts of, well he might not be living here or anywhere else for much longer, sped through my brain. I felt a combination of guilt and relief for a few seconds. Then I said. "Sorry, I didn't mean to startle you. I was only coming in to get something to eat."

"Looks like you got a lot of food in here. Did you cook all this?" he asked.

"No. Most of that casserole stuff is left-overs from the funeral dinner."

"So. You had lots of people here to give you food."

"Grandpa had a lot of friends."

"Yeah. I remember. No matter what anybody says you only get one dad in this life. You don't have any beer do you?"

"Not unless someone besides me put it in there."

"You might be an adult but you won't be able to buy beer for another five years."

"Seven"

"Seven what?"

"Seven years, I'm fourteen."

"Oh yeah. Big for your age aren't you? The old man must have fed you pretty good. What do you weigh son?"

"The school locker room scale says a hundred and eighty-eight when the doctor's office scale reads a hundred and ninety. You tell me."

"Close enough for me either way. Ever get in any fights?"

"Nope."

"Uh-huh. You want something to eat you said right?"

"Yeah, I'll probably have some of that leftover spaghetti some lady friend of grandpa's brought."

"She brought enough of it didn't she? The only place I've seen a bowl that big is when I eat at the church."

"You eat at the church?"

"Kid, I've enjoyed a free meal in quite a few different places. I'll have to tell you about it someday. Right now I'd really go for a beer."

"Is there any in the fridge?" I asked.

"Is there?"

"No," I said.

"Is there a fridge in the garage with beer in it?"

"No."

He closed the refrigerator door.

We stood silently in the kitchen for what seemed way too long.

"I need to get in the fridge for some of that spaghetti," I said.

He nodded at me then he walked out into the dining room.

I got my food ready. I scooped out the last three big spoonfuls of spaghetti and meat balls from the big bowl onto a dinner plate. Then I put the plate into the microwave to heat up the food for a minute as I made a mental note to make some mac and cheese tomorrow. My dad was quiet in the living room while I listened to the whir of the electric motor and fan of the microwave. The oven beeped once at me. I opened the door to shut off the beeper then I reached in to turn my plate halfway round, closed the oven again then reset the timer for another minute. While the microwave worked to heat up my dinner I ran hot water in the sink, put in the dish soap then placed the empty pasta bowl into the hot soapy water. When the minute passed by the oven beeped again. I opened the door to find my pasta was steaming hot. I smiled.

It had been a long time since lunch and what seemed a much longer time since I got home to find my dad waiting to move in with me. He wasn't making a sound in the living room. When I finished eating and cleaning up I went into the living room to discover he had fallen asleep on the couch while lying on his left side. His head rested on the arm rest while his right arm rested on his belly. His left hand lay limp, nearly touching the ground. He was breathing with his mouth open. He was also drooling saliva onto the couch. He was drooling in his sleep. His drooling reminded me of Maximus being such a slobber dog.

I thought now that he's drooled on my couch I have to let him stay; because, that has to be his spot from now on. At that moment I resolved to never sit on that part of the couch again. I went into the kitchen to do my homework until it was time to get ready for bed. When I was done I went into the living room.

I looked out at Maximus in the front yard. Sometimes I let him sleep in the house, but most nights I liked it when he was standing guard on the front porch as he usually did before he lay down to sleep for the night. My dad was snoring on the couch where I had left him earlier. I went to the bathroom to get ready for bed. I took a shower, brushed my teeth, went to the bathroom, then I walked into my bedroom where I put on my pajamas.

When I got in bed I left the light on for a while. I kept looking up at the ceiling where I could see all kinds of shapes in the dry-wall texture. For me it was like looking up at the clouds in a summer sky as they changed shape right before your eyes. Looking at the texture was kind of like that for me. I discovered I could imagine the various combinations of the unmoving texture shapes to be pretty much anything I wanted. It also reminded me of looking up at the night sky, connecting the stars to make anything you wanted. In school we learned the old time Greeks used to do that by thinking stars were all kinds of things, bears, crabs and the like. I look up at the stars to see things way different than they did. I think it must have been a lot darker at night two or three thousand years ago. Anyway, I did this a lot after my grandpa died.

I went in bed to lay down so I could look up with my eyes to let my mind wander through my bedroom ceiling sky. I imagined going to lots of places I had never been before. Now that my dad was here I thought maybe I'd be going lots of new imaginary places.

I woke up to my alarm at my regular six am wake-up time. I was surprised to have slept through the night. My dad must have slept pretty well. When I went out to see where he was I found him still sleeping on the couch where grandpa had died. He was dressed in the same clothes he had on when I was talking to him the night before. He was sleeping soundly. His mouth was open. I could see the top side of his tongue. It looked like the drool had come from under the bottom side of his tongue. There was a little puddle on the couch cushion. I went to the bathroom. Cleaned myself and got dressed. I went to the kitchen to get some breakfast. I put some Cheerios in a bowl with milk. Topped the cereal with a sliced banana. I also made two toasts, one with peanut butter, and one with strawberry jelly.

I left my dad sleeping. He didn't even wake up when I took the D-35 and its stand into grandpa's room. I wanted the guitar in its case so I could stash it in the closet with his other guitar gear. Other than having my dad in the house on the couch I didn't know quite what I wanted to do with him. I always enjoyed eating my meals in peace. I didn't want to get into some kind of disagreement with him. I didn't know if I would or not. I didn't want to take the chance.

I got ready for school. My dad never stirred when I left for school. On my way out I fed and watered Maximus. As I fed him I asked him. "Do you think my dad will be here when I come home?" Maximus looked up at me then looked down into his bowl to keep on eating. He did not give me an answer either way. "Yeah like you're going to be giving me any advice," I said to him. "I wish grandpa was here so I could listen to him tell me how to handle my dad like he handled him before."

I walked, like I almost always did, the almost a mile to Franklin Middle school. Things were almost the same. School was all the same. I wasn't quite the same. I found myself preoccupied with thinking about lots of things, including my dad. My math teacher

Mr. Herndon asked me why I seemed a bit distracted. I told him I was thinking about things. He let it go at that. He knew my grandpa had recently died. I don't know what my teacher had in his mind. I figured he thought I was thinking about my grandpa being gone.

The thing is I was thinking about all of us, my grandpa, my dad, and me. I wondered how my dad got to be the way he was when his dad was such a good person. I thought about that a lot. Also I wanted to know why I wasn't important enough to my dad for him to take care of me as a kid. I wondered a lot about a lot of things. By the time school was over it seemed like the day had flown past like a jet. I went through the motions, but there was a lot I must have missed. I couldn't wait to get home to see what I would find. I walked home as I usually did.

When I got to where I could see the front yard at my house I noticed Maximus was chained up to a post or something that had been stuck into the front lawn. As I got near to the fence I could see Maximus had walked around with the chain so many times he was lying down about a foot away from what looked like a wooden stick. He was stuck. When I got into the yard to set him free I could see the stick was an old yellow wooden broom handle pounded into the ground. The chain was knotted up so that Maximus was forced to stay near the old handle. I put my backpack full of books down on the ground then untied him. He was panting more than usual. He didn't have any food or water close enough to him so he could eat or get a drink. He walked slowly over to his water bowl. I watched him drink like he hadn't had a drink all day. Even for him it was a lot of water. I didn't see any sign of my dad outside. I went in the house.

The door was unlocked. The TV was on. My dad was sleeping on the couch as if he hadn't moved from where I had seen him in the morning. Except for the beer bottles on the floor next to the couch and the half empty bottle of whiskey on the end table it looked as if he hadn't moved all day. Obviously he had moved as much as he needed to get drunk enough to go back to sleep. I turned the TV off. Then I stood there for a few seconds deciding what to do. I felt really sad. I went into the kitchen to put my books on the table then I went into my bedroom to lay down on my bed. I looked up at the ceiling. The textured geography of my bedroom ceiling, where I imagined I was looking at what might have been a desert seen from an airplane or a spaceship like the shuttle orbiting the earth, was still there for me to make into anything I wanted it to be. I let my mind wander for a while. I'm not sure how long. Pretty soon I heard my dad making some sounds like he was moving around. A little huffing and puffing meant he must be getting up, sitting up, or at least moving. All of a sudden he yelled at me.

"Daryl! Is that you?" he asked.

"I can hear you," I said. Then I got up and walked out into the living room.

"What time is it?" he asked.

I looked at the ticking clock on the wall that hung about three feet above the TV. The colorful clock grandpa bought years ago had pictures of various song birds doing their individual calls on the hour. They had ceased doing that quite a while ago. The clock kept good time though, even without the singing birds.

"It's about five-fifteen. See there's a clock there on the wall," I said as I pointed it out for him.

"Oh yeah. I forgot to look," he said. "Did you turn off the TV?"

"Yeah, you were sleeping. It's almost time for dinner. Are you hungry?" I asked.

He put his hand near his stomach like he had done before.

"Nah, I'm not hungry. I got a gut ache today."

"I'm going to make some mac and cheese. Grandpa's friend taught me how to fix up a box of that stuff with some added extras. It comes out pretty good," I said. Then I gave him a big smile.

"Well you're pretty pleased with your damn self about that mac and cheese concoction are you?" he said.

"It's pretty good," I said.

"If you like that sort of thing."
"Yeah, I guess so."
"Not hungry," he said.
"Okay, well I am. So I'm going to get something to eat."
"Okay, well, I'm going to stay right here."

As I went into the kitchen I could hear that he turned the TV on.

"Hey kid bring me a beer from the fridge," he said.

I opened the fridge. Where some leftovers had been he had stuffed in what looked like a whole shelf of beer cans. I laughed a little when I saw it because I thought Homer Simpson must have filled my fridge.

I took two of the cold cans to him in the living room.

"Well there's a real smart boy. Bringing two instead of only one. Smart boy," he said.

I gave my dad another big smile. While I thought: You're my dad and you've got a lot of problems. I don't think you're going to be staying in my house for very long. Especially if this is how you live your life.

I stopped smiling as I stood there looking at him. He opened both beer cans with a crack and hiss. As he took a big long drink from one of them he looked at me. He had his head tilted back as he gulped down beer. He gave me a side long glance then he coughed trying to swallow. He put the first beer can which looked to be empty, because he put it down on its side, next to the full one, on the card table he had positioned in front of the couch. Then he shook his head.

"What are you staring at boy?" He asked me. Then he said: "And wipe that self-satisfied smile off your big dumb face. Stop staring at me like you're some kind of a needy cow."

I rolled my eyes, closed them for a couple of seconds then turned to walk back into the kitchen. I felt more sadness than anything else. I thought, that's my dad. No wonder my grandpa took me in.

I got out all the stuff I needed to make mac and cheese, the flour, milk, seasonings, the cheese and noodles. One of grandpa's female friends showed me how to make a roux. How to season it just right with a little black pepper, table salt and her secret ingredient, a pinch of smoked paprika. She told me how to mix it, to put in the right amount of flour and milk. How to make it real creamy by using evaporated milk instead of regular milk. As I was heating up the roux in grandpa's favorite old all aluminum Wearever saucepan I listened to my dad making various noises in the living room.

I could hear the TV. I couldn't hear everything he was doing, but I could hear him swear a little, laugh a little, then he coughed his nasty sounding cough. I thought he was going to hack a lung up onto the floor. I don't know what he'd been watching. Whatever it was made him laugh enough to make him cough. I figured maybe that's why he doesn't laugh much. I finished boiling up the elbow macaroni, combined all the ingredients into a covered glass dish then put it in the oven. Pretty soon I didn't hear my dad at all. When I went to see why all I could hear was the TV. I found him sleeping again.

I turned off the TV. I didn't like much of what was on TV. TV was about people I didn't know so I didn't pay that much attention to it. Even the news was so filled with bad stuff that made me sad I hardly watched it. But, there was my dad so mesmerized by it all it put him to sleep, again. I guess that's what must have happened to him. Either that or he passed out from drinking. I'm not sure which. Probably a little of both.

I went back into the kitchen to do some homework on the red Formica topped chrome-legged table grandpa had gotten when some club he played in remodeled. I timed the mac and cheese to my school work. When my homework was done I knew the mac and cheese would be ready. Sometimes I overcooked it a little to get the cheese crusty on top. While I was eating I could hear my dad snoring. He got a bit louder for a while then he stopped snoring altogether. I worried about him dying on the same couch where my grandpa had died so I got up right away to look at him.

I went into the living room so I could look him over. I thought maybe he was dead. I leaned down next to him. He had rolled a little onto his left side which changed the sound of his breathing. He wasn't snoring anymore, but he was still alive. What would I do if he up and died on me? He sure looked like he could. He looked nearly as old as grandpa, but way less healthy. He was skinny except for having a big belly. His body looked kind of distorted. His belly was way too big for the rest of him.

So there he was, my dad. Lying on my couch, drooling again, not much, but a little. He looked worn out like some old used car with a million miles on it that nobody ever took care of. If he had been a car, he looked like he could have been in a bunch of destruction derbies and lost, every time. To me his breath smelled like sulfuric acid, stale beer, rancid pancake syrup and who knew what else? Stuff that had all been oozing together in his stomach to create some kind of a radioactive slurry which when he wanted to talk, he could command to come forth from within him as a kind of toxic volcanic-like smoke, that would flow between and past his rotten teeth from out of the chimney of his throat. His farts were worse. He coughed and wheezed, his arms and legs were thin, with a few scars here and there. I was scared to see what he looked like naked. I don't know how he was still alive.

Having my dad in my house made me think about my mom. My mom had not been in my life for as long as I could remember. I was six when grandpa told me my mom died. When I was six I didn't really get it. I was small and hadn't ever known her. The fact that no one seemed to know exactly how old she was when she died didn't make sense to me. If she had died in her early twenties she must have had me when she was in her late teens. She was quite a few years younger than my dad, ten or fifteen or something like that. Grandpa had shown me some old black and white pictures of her he had taken with his ancient Zeiss film camera. In the pictures my mom looked beautiful. My dad was a good looking guy too. But, not anymore. I wondered how my mom looked when she died. If she really died by shooting up some bad heroin she was poisoned, so I hope it didn't hurt when she died. Grandpa never told me what happened to her body. I decided to ask my dad sometime. Maybe I could go visit her at a cemetery. The more I thought about my mom the quieter I got inside. I found it hard to not feel as much as I thought I ought to feel for her, about her, or however, or whatever I expected I didn't know. What I did know about my mom and dad didn't help me much.

Maximus started barking. I looked out the window toward the cyclone fence next to the sidewalk at a man who quickly backed away from the fence as he kept staring at Maximus who was making his fear inducing bark. The man was well dressed. He was wearing a man's fancy hat, not a derby, but, another kind I didn't know the name of, but I think it started with an F. Maybe it was called federal, or something. Anyway, I thought it looked gangster like. He was wearing a grey suit the same color as his hat. He was carrying some kind of leather satchel in his left hand. From the way he was acting I knew he wasn't going to try to come in the yard as long as Maximus was there.

My dad woken up by Maximus yelled at me. "Shut up that damn dog. Can't you control that mutt?"

I opened the door then stepped outside. Maximus looked at me then back at the man. As I walked out to the gate I told the man. "It's okay he won't hurt you if you don't do anything quick around me." Which was my favorite line to tell people I didn't know when they came to my house. It worked really good to keep them from getting too close.

"Quite the dog you've got there," the man said.

"Yeah"

"Sir my name is David Williams. I am here to inquire as to the whereabouts of a Mr. Daryl Brown."

"Oh?" I asked.

"Yes sir. Do you know Daryl Brown, or how I can get into contact with Mr. Brown?"

"I don't know who you are."

"Like I said my name is David Williams. I am trying to contact Mr. Daryl Brown. I can only talk to him about the nature of my business with him."

"How come?"

"I am sorry sir. At this time I can't reveal that to anyone except Mr. Brown. Perhaps you can tell me if I have the correct address for him?"

I glanced back up at the house. It was all quiet. The door was closed. I didn't see my dad anywhere near the windows.

"This is the right address. Are you trying to sell me something?"

"You? Are you Daryl Brown?"

"As long as this isn't some kind of trick or something. Which I can let Maximus take care of for me," I said. Then I pointed to my St. Bernard who was sitting next to me as I talked to the man who was standing quietly on the concrete sidewalk about ten feet away from me. There was a small pool of slick saliva spreading on the concrete near my dog's front feet.

"No Daryl, can I call you Daryl? I can assure you it's not a trick," he asked.

"Yeah, sure."

"I will need to see some kind of photographic personal identification of you to verify that what you are telling me is true in order for me to give you what I was sent to hand deliver to you."

"Hand deliver?"

"Yes, Mr. Brown. I am from an insurance company where your grandfather had a policy."

"I have someone in the house I don't want to know things about me. How about if I go get my ID and show you out here?"

"If that's what you want to do."

"Maximus, come here boy," I said to make Maximus follow me to the house. "Wait here on the porch."

As quietly as I could I went in the house.

"What the hell's going on?" my dad yelled.

"I'm not sure. It's some salesman or something," I said.

"Tell him to get out of here then."

"I will," I said as I kept walking to my bedroom to get my identification card from my wallet. When I went back outside Maximus walked with me to the fence. I reached over the fence to show the man my ID. He looked at the card, looked up at me, and then gave me a big smile.

"Thank you so much Mr. Brown.," he said as he opened his fat leather satchel to retrieve an envelope.

"This is the beneficiary check for you from your grandfather's life insurance policy. I am sorry I had to be so reluctantly secretive about giving it to you. We, my company and I, must be sure we are giving these benefits to the correct person," he said.

I took the envelope from him with my right hand. "So this is for me?" I asked.

"Yes sir. You are your grandfather's sole named beneficiary. If I was to give you some ideas of what to do with that check I'd advise you not to tell anyone about it except an attorney you trust and perhaps a financial adviser. I want to thank you for your grandfather's trust in our company. Here is my card if I can be of further assistance to you. Good day Mr. Brown," he said. Then he tipped his hat to me before he began walking away.

"Hey mister," I called out after him.

He turned toward me. He was about twenty feet away.

"I'm sorry for being so suspicious of you," I said.

"I'm glad you were. You need to know who you are dealing with. There are too many scammers, tricksters, and con artists in the world. Like I said, my advice to you is to talk to an attorney you trust. Your grandfather's attorney would probably be a good choice."

"Thanks."

"You are welcome young man. I wish you the best. Do something good with what your grandfather has left to you."

"Okay, thanks."

"Goodbye."

"Yeah, goodbye."

He smiled at me then turned to continue walking down the street.

Before turning around to face the house I tucked the long white envelope into the front of my pants so I could cover it with my shirt. Maximus sniffed at my shirt as per his usual inquisitive self to see what I had. I walked back up to the house, told Maximus to stay outside, then I went in.

"What the hell took you so long to get rid of a salesman?" dad asked.

"I don't know."

"Is there something you're not telling your old man Daryl?"

"I got him to go away didn't I?"

"Why don't you go study or something? Make sure you keep that slobber machine outside too. Can't you see I'm trying to take a nap here?"

I responded by walking silently to my bedroom. I made like I was getting out my books and papers so my dad would think I was obeying him. I hated the way he talked about Maximus. I shut my bedroom door. I took out the insurance company envelope from my shirt. Inside the envelope was a cashier's check made out to me, Daryl Brown. The amount of the check was four-hundred-sixty-three-thousand dollars and forty-two cents.

I looked at that check for what seemed like a pretty long time. I had never seen a cashier's check before. I had never seen a check for such a huge amount of money either. I put it back in the envelope in which it had come. Then I took it out again to look at it. Then I put it back in the envelope. Then I took it out again. I put it back in the envelope. I took it out once again. I slowly put it back in the envelope while I tried to think of a place to hide it. I knew I had to deposit it in the bank soon. I couldn't tell anyone I had that much money. Especially not my dad.

I went out to the living room to see if my dad was still sleeping. He had turned on the TV, but for some reason kept it on mute.

"So what do you want Daryl?" he asked.

"I don't want anything. I wanted to see if you were hungry for some dinner," I said.

He looked right at me and said, "No."

"Okay"

"So, what were you really doing coming out here?" he asked. "Wanted to see if I was awake did you? Are you going to have some of your non-existent friends over?" he said.

"I have friends," I said.

He nodded at me then said, "Sure you do. You got all kinds of friends. You just don't want them to come over while I'm here is that it?"

The truth is he was right. I had friends, they were all at school. Since my grandpa had died I hadn't wanted to be very social. I had really wanted to be by myself. I really missed my grandpa. I wished he hadn't died. I knew grandpa was the best friend I could ever have.

"Grandpa was my best friend," I said.

He looked at me with a blank stare. Then he smirked as he shook his head back and forth. He looked away from me as he held up his left hand. He flipped his left hand at me to dismiss me.

I went back in my room without saying anything. I wanted to do something to get rid of him. I needed to know. How to get rid of my deadbeat dad? He was getting booze and beer somehow. I decided to stay home from school in the morning. I would be sick for the day. That way maybe I could find out how he was getting his liquor. I wasn't hungry anymore so I did homework in my room then got ready for bed and went to sleep.

Dogs, Cars, and Old Men

In the morning I decided to carry out my sick plan. I got out the old fashioned mercury thermometer grandpa had, rolled it in my hands to increase the temperature reading. I got it to read a hundred and two point six. I went to show my dad who was still lying on the couch. He was out cold. I shook him awake. Then I told him.

"Hey, I'm sick. I've got a fever. I'm staying home today."

"Stay away from me. I don't want you making me sick," he said.

He had glanced at the thermometer, but didn't look to see what the temperature was. I went back to my room. I lay down on my bed to look at the textured ceiling so I could let my mind wander to help me think. I started seeing things I usually saw, faces, animals, stuff like that. I decided to stay in bed for a while. I wanted to know what to do with that big check. Now that I was faking sick I figured I probably ought to stay home and not go to a bank. I wanted to figure out what to do with this drunken man, my dad. I fell asleep. The phone woke me up. I could hear my dad answer it. He was talking, but I couldn't quite make out what he was saying. I got up to go into the kitchen. He looked up at me as I passed by.

"Shush, I got to take care of something. I'll have to call you back." He said before he hung up.

"That was none of your business kid," he said to me.

I shrugged as I continued into the kitchen, making like I didn't care what he said. I could see the bird clock was reading a little after ten am.

Since I wasn't actually sick I had to act the part which I wasn't very good at. I made myself some toast and eggs like I often did. While I was cooking I could feel some tension in the house. I felt a little queasy now. He was coming into the kitchen.

"Sick huh?"

I nodded yes while I was eating my eggs and toast.

"You staying home all day?"

I nodded again.

"What did you do with that old guitar?" he asked.

"I put it back in its case," I said.

He nodded, then quietly said, "Okay."

I stopped eating.

He was standing next to the table. "Okay, that was a good idea. That's a nice guitar your grandpa has," he said.

I nodded again.

He knocked softly on the table once with the knuckles of his right hand then turned quickly around to walk toward the bathroom.

That was all we ever said about grandpa's guitars.

I felt pretty sure that we both knew I wasn't actually sick. He didn't keep after me about it though. There was developing a kind of complicity with what each of us was doing that the other one didn't want the other one to know. He knew I wasn't being forthright. I knew he wasn't being forthright. Neither of us wanted to admit anything to each other. That was how we were both able to keep our lives separate. I didn't really understand that at the time even though I knew how to not tell him stuff I didn't want him to know. That way I wasn't lying on purpose. I just didn't tell him much about what I was doing. At the time I also needed to do something with all that money so he wouldn't know anything about it. I didn't trust him. I figured he would go through my room whenever I wasn't home.

He spent what seemed like a much longer time than he usually did in the bathroom. Then he came back into the kitchen.

"So. An associate of mine will be coming over here sometime today or this evening. We're going to be spending some time associating with each other. You aren't invited," he said.

"Let me know when they're coming. I'll hide in my bedroom, in my house."

"Yeah, good idea," he said.

I looked around the living room where my dad spent most of his time. He had pretty much taken over the house by taking over the living room. Both of us avoided going into grandpa's room. I had my room; which, I preferred over all the rooms in the house. It had always been where I spent most of my time at home. So I went to my room to lay down on my bed for a while. I wanted to figure out what to do with the check the insurance man had given me. By the time I lay down on my bed to look at my ceiling I started thinking not only of the money grandpa had left me, but my overall situation with my dad.

When grandpa was alive he pretty much had all the rest of the house to himself except my room. He always inspected my room to see what I had in there. He didn't want me doing or having anything I wasn't supposed to. It was like my dad had replaced my grandpa as the person having the most space available to them in the house. It wasn't like my dad used all the space in the house, he just filled it by being there. I mean his being in the living room meant I had to see him when I went in or out of the kitchen or out the front door, or down the hall from one room to the other. I think the thing that made it seem like he was in the whole house was his smell. He stunk. I don't know how often or if he bathed or showered at all. I had washed a few more wash cloths than usual but not any extra towels since he arrived.

I think the worst thing that happened to me since my dad showed up was how oblivious he seemed about how he affected me. Since he spent most of each day and night on the couch he kind of controlled all the space in the house. It didn't take me long to figure out that my dad wasn't someone who cleaned up after himself either. He draped clothes on furniture, left his socks in his shoes when he wasn't wearing them. He piled up dirty dishes on the card table in front of the couch as well as both lamp tables at each end of the couch. He didn't seem to eat a whole lot though so there weren't that many dishes. He always had one of grandpa's Grand Canyon Coffee mugs with some kind of liquid besides coffee in it sitting on the end table at the head end of the couch. I named the ends of the couch the foot end and the head end, because he always had his feet at the end of the couch nearest the kitchen, while the head end was in more of a direct line to the TV. He seemed to spend most of his time watching TV while he drank some kind of alcohol.

To me he never seemed like he was drunk. I thought drunk people talked weird or got crazy or something. He almost always seemed to be the same. Which was kind of irritated and kind of sneaky, all at the same time.

It wasn't the living room alone that got dirtier and messier. It was like he dragged messiness around him like a disease. Wherever he went got out of order. I could tell when he had been in any room besides the living room; because, it was in disarray of some kind. If he had been in the bathroom the toilet paper would be hanging down touching the floor, the toilet would need flushing if all he did was pee. He only flushed if he crapped. The towels would be mashed together on the rack so they couldn't dry. There would be a wash cloth or two on the floor. Sometimes I found big loogies stuck in the sink that he didn't bother to wash down. For as much time as he spent in the bathroom he never seemed to smell any cleaner. He always seemed dirty to me. It was his smell that followed him everywhere and hung in the air after he left a room. I found myself washing my hands after pulling on the sticky refrigerator handle; because, when I opened the fridge my hand felt like there was some kind of dirty film on the handle. I washed my hands then the handle. After my dad touched things they felt dirty to me.

After being in the house a while the smell didn't seem quite so bad. I think that was because of what my science teacher told my class after a stinky demonstration she did at the front of the lab room went wrong. All of us kids had to go outside for safety. She told us if we stayed in the classroom for more than forty-five seconds we wouldn't be able to smell the stench she had created at the lab table. So we all trooped out the sliding glass side door that allowed easy access to outside in case of situations like that to stand on the grass while the danger went away. We were all still standing there when the fire department came to put out the little fire that was starting to erupt from whatever chemicals she had incorrectly combined to show us something. What she showed us was way different than she had intended. The next day when we came to class there was a lingering odor in the science lab that wasn't there before her messed up experiment.

That was the way it was with my house. There was a smell that didn't want to go away. When I had been gone for a while, even outside for a few minutes, then went back into my house I noticed it way more. After I had been there a little while it wasn't so smelly. I guess that had to be the forty-five second thing that our noses do. My science teacher told us our noses alert us to a stink. That we should pay attention to our nose alert. If we don't pay attention to our nose then stay in the stinky place we're doomed to have to suffer from the toxic effect of the smell without knowing it's there.

My house was quickly turning into a dirty stinky mess. As my dad became more and more comfortable in my house, the house itself was turning into the den of an alcoholic badger or bear or some other smelly animal that drank liquor.

I didn't want to be doomed to smell my stinky dad the rest of my life. Still I didn't want to try to figure out how to get a grown man, my father, to not live like some kind of smelly animal. That was wrong. I shouldn't be the person trying to get my dad to grow up. I was the kid. He was supposed to be the man, the father. My father was living in my house. I admitted to myself I wanted some kind of relationship with my long lost dad. I had been putting up with anything to have him back. I didn't know how long I could live with him like he was though.

For my fake sick day I hung out at home. I got up and ate a couple of times. All I ever saw or heard my dad do was go to the bathroom, watch TV or talk on the phone. I couldn't hear hardly anything he said. He talked real quiet into the receiver except for one time he swore loud at someone before slamming down the phone. I played the sick card all day on into the evening. I fed Maximus outside then I brought him into my bedroom for a while. My dad always complained about Maximus. He said Maximus had started growling at him so he threw a shoe at him. I had noticed Maximus giving a low growl at my dad whenever my dad talked loud to me. I didn't really find out what was going on with Maximus and my dad. It seemed like my dad hardly ever ate real food. He also didn't clean up after himself. I don't think he ever washed his hands after going to the bathroom. I heard the toilet flush once in a while although I never heard water running in the sink after he went to the bathroom.

I got caught up on my homework before I cleaned up my room real good. I had my check hidden in my school work where I figured my dad would never look. I went to bed early for me, about eight pm. I fell asleep reading.

I woke up groggy. My night light was on. I looked over at my clock. It was two forty-five in the morning. I could hear talking in the living room. That must have been what woke me up I said softly to myself. It seemed really loud to hear my own voice at that time of night. I rolled onto my back to listen to whatever I could hear.

It seemed like my dad was talking to someone. Or he was talking to the TV. It could have been either one. Then I heard a woman laugh. At least it sounded like a woman. I got out of bed as quietly as I could then tip-toed down the hall to sneak a peek from the dark hallway to see what was going on in the living room. The TV was on. I could hear my dad talking with someone. Definitely a woman was talking back to him. I stopped short of the entry to the living room so I could listen to them. They sounded awfully chummy. Then I guessed they were having some kind of sex right there on the couch where my grandpa had died. My stomach got kind of tight, I felt a little like throwing up. How could they do that? Well I guess I was the only one except for the funeral home people who knew grandpa had died right there where my dad had been sleeping. Now my dad was having sex there. I decided to peek at them to be sure that what I was hearing was what I thought was happening.

I stuck my head out a bit around the corner. The light was coming from the TV. There was a woman facing the TV who looked like she was sitting on my dad's lap. She wasn't sitting still though. She had her hands on her knees as she rocked back and forth. She had some really big breasts swinging back and forth against her body. My dad was sitting on the edge of the couch as he leaned back into the cushions. They were definitely doing it. They didn't notice me at all so I watched for a while. I was standing in the dark. They couldn't have seen me even if they looked my way. Fortunately they weren't looking my way.

As I watched them I could see they had been drinking alcohol. There were beer cans on the floor. I could smell hard liquor too. They made some heavy breathing sounds. I thought for a while my dad was going to have a heart attack. He heaved up and down on the couch a few times then fell back into the couch like he was too heavy for his body. The woman was laughing as she hoisted herself up off my dad. She turned around to stand facing him. She looked down at him in what I thought seemed like triumph. She was acting like she had won something. She asked my dad, "So, what do you think of that Mister Brown?"

My dad was still trying to catch his breath. He was huffing and puffing like he was going to die any second. There was this woman, I had never seen before, standing over him like she had just beat him across the finish line in some kind of race. She was more naked than any real woman I had ever seen. I couldn't look away from her body. She had long wavy dark looking hair. When she shook her head to let her hair hang down her back she sent her large breasts lolling across her chest. She had kind of a puffy stomach area that matched her breasts. She was not a tall woman. I thought she had a pretty big belly for her height. I kept looking at her big moving breasts when I realized they were pointing directly at me. I could see she was leaning forward as if she was trying to see me. When she did that her breasts hung down away from her body.

"Who's there?" she said.

I was so startled I froze where I was.

"What the hell?" my dad said.

"I thought you said this was your house and we'd be all alone. What kind of thing are you trying to pull here Bertrand? You got somebody sitting in the dark with a camera trying to film me?" She said.

Still breathing hard my dad yelled at me, "Get the hell to bed Daryl."

"Daryl? Who the hell is Daryl?"

"He's my son."

"You got a camera boy?" she said.

"No ma'am. I was just looking" I said.

She put a hand under each of her breasts to point them right at me. "Get a good look sonny. These are some of the world's best looking breasts you'll never see again," she said.

Then she laughed out loud.

My dad sat on the couch with his breaths coming a little slower.

I got a real good look at her breasts in that dim light. I could see her a lot better than she could see me. I could even see a patch of hair between the top of her legs.

"Get out here boy so I can see you," she said.

"No, I don't want to."

"Come out here boy," she said.

I stepped around the corner from the hallway into the living room.

"You're a big one aren't you? Did you have your hand down your pants while me and your dad was having a go?"

"What? No, I didn't" I said.

"Well maybe later you'll be inspired," she said as she was pulling on her underwear panties.

She finished dressing, bra, jeans, blouse, shoes, before she spoke again.

My dad had his eyes closed.

She looked at me then pointed her right thumb at my dad. Then she said. "He's about done in you know. I'm surprised he made it through that session without permanently blowing a gasket. I'm not dating him anymore. I was married to a guy who died on top of me. Ever since then I stay on top. All men think they're invincible. Remember that kid. You're not invincible. You can put money on that."

I smiled. She had let me see her naked, watch her dress herself as if she was looking in a mirror, and gave me advice while she did it. I liked her, a lot.

"What about me?" I asked.

"What about you what?" she said.

"What you did to my dad?"

She laughed out loud again.

"Why not? I'm emancipated."

"You're what?"

"Emancipated. It means I can take care of myself."

"As big as you are kid I'm sure you're right," she said. Then she kissed me square on the lips and said. "Not tonight anyway honey. I've had enough of one Mr. Brown for this evening. You think about Laura later, when you're alone. Then remember I'm old enough to be your grandma. Think about that when you're thinking about me."

I stopped thinking about her body and started realizing she was kind of an old woman. When she kissed me her lips were moist, kind of waxy. She smelled sweaty as well as sweet and sour, kind of like Chinese food I'd had. The smell made me a little hungry.

"Hey, Bertrand," she said. "Don't die tonight. I'd feel bad if I had anything to do with pleasuring you out of this world. I'll let myself out."

She headed over to open the front door. When she opened it Maximus came in and walked over to me. I don't know why but he didn't bark. My dad raised his right hand over his head then let it drop to make like he was sending her away, dismissing her like he did me. She laughed again, then let the screen door shut behind her. I went over to close the house door as well as to watch her walk away. I watched her lilt her way down the sidewalk. After she let herself out the gate she began to walk down the street. I watched her until she was at the end of my fence then I closed the front door.

My dad was snoring when I went to check on him. He was a mess, his shirt was wide open, and his pants were down around his knees. He was bathed in sweat, nearly naked, and as usual he was stinky. He looked like a rag doll attacked by a dog. I put a blanket over him then I went to bed in my own room.

I remembered what that woman's body looked like. It made me smile to know I had seen a grown woman naked. I thought she was really sexy. I can't say I thought she was pretty. She was way too old for me. I surprised myself thinking a woman as old as her could seem so sexy. Grandpa told me the things I needed to know about the differences between men and women; however, grandpa never had any women come to visit him for anything like my dad had been doing. Grandpa didn't even have any men's magazines that I knew of. Grandpa was pretty dignified about bodies, sex and the like. He always taught me that sex was for married people. That it was a private thing for people who loved each other so they could express their love for one another.

He also told me about making babies and how that worked. But he only did that after I had a class in school with presentations given by medical people who explained pretty much everything in detail except for how it felt. They never told me how I would feel when a naked woman pointed her big bare breasts at me. Or how I would feel when she told me it was off limits to do anything with her. So when I thought about how she looked, how different it was for me to feel what I felt. Seeing a movie about something or hearing someone talk about something isn't nearly the same thing like they show you in school. We saw a movie. Then someone tried to explain the movie. I thought they should have been at my house tonight to know what sex was really like. It was wild, scary, exciting, weird, and exhilarating all at the same time.

I lay there in bed waiting to hear if my dad was okay. I didn't feel like looking at him anymore so I was relieved when I could hear him snoring, and snorting. After I fell asleep thinking about what I had seen I woke up with a mess in my pajama pants again. That wasn't new for me. That had happened quite a bit in the last couple of years. I slipped out of my pajamas so I could clean myself up. I wiped off with them then rolled them up with the mess in the middle so I could drop them on the floor for the morning laundry.

My room was dark, quiet. I couldn't hear my Dad. I lay there wondering when I would have sex. Grandpa always told me it was better to wait till you were married. When I asked him if he had sex before he got married he admitted he had sex before he met grandma. He also said marrying grandma was the best thing he ever did. He told me he wished he had only ever made love to her.

I had asked my dad's girlfriend that night if she would do with me what she had done with my dad. I might have had sex for the first time if she hadn't told me no. I think she might have done it with me if she knew how rich I was. I was falling asleep thinking about these things. I wanted to do it with her. I wished I had and I was glad I hadn't. I know I wanted to. I know I wanted sex with someone. I wanted sex. I was a free man. Maybe it was about time. I wondered if being emancipated meant I could get married. I woke up to my dad having a coughing fit. He went back to snoring. I listened to him till I went back to sleep.

When I woke up I took my dirty pajamas into the bathroom to put them in the clothes hamper grandpa always kept there behind the door. I looked at myself in the mirror. I decided, then said out loud to myself like grandpa taught me to do, "I'm good enough looking to have a girlfriend."

Those were some of the things grandpa told me to do. If I felt bad about myself for any reason he used to tell me "Daryl, you go look at your best self in the mirror and tell yourself you're a healthy, smart, good looking young man capable of whatever you set your mind to. Tell yourself you're not going to sell yourself short no matter what anyone else says about you. Always remember you are a child of God who made you to do good things in this world for yourself and everybody else. It doesn't matter that other people don't do what you do. You do things right the best you can. You love people like God does and you will have a great life. God loves everybody even when they don't love God back. That's what you have the opportunity to do Daryl. I can guarantee you will live a full blessed life if you do that."

I did that this morning. Looked at myself in the mirror and said, "Daryl," then I couldn't help smiling at the memory of my grandpa, "you got everything you need to have a great life. You are a good looking strong man who can take care of himself. You will find the right girl for you." I pushed my chest out like grandpa said so I would feel courageous. I felt it. Now, what about my dad I asked myself in the mirror?

He was still asleep on the couch. The blanket I draped over him was still there, like he hadn't moved all night. He looked like grandpa lying there with his eyes closed. Except he still looked sick to me. He seemed washed out looking, like he was real tired. He sounded like it too. His belly looked like it might be bigger than it was a couple days ago. I thought Laura could be right. He might not live much longer. My mom was dead, my grandpa and grandma were both dead. If he died I really would be emancipated. I would be all alone.

I didn't want to be alone.

I got a shower and got ready for school. I got my insurance check to take with me. My dad slept through everything I did. That is until Maximus started his "I want to go out," bark. Anytime I slept in forgetting to put Maximus out he would remind me he had to go out for his early morning duty. I let Maximus out the front door then looked over at my dad. His eyes were pretty much open, but he wasn't looking at me. He didn't say anything to me.

"I'm heading out to school. Are you going to be okay?"

He motioned me with his right arm like he had done to Laura. It was his just-go-away wave.

I closed the unlocked door to let the screen door slam on its own. I forgot to water Maximus earlier so I stopped. I put my bag down on the walk as I went back into the house for a pitcher of water to fill Maximus's bowl. When I went to fill the bowl I saw a few beer cans I hadn't seen before littering the front lawn. They were the kind my dad drank. I don't know how he paid for anything. I don't think he was stealing from me. I wasn't missing any money, at least that I knew of. Maybe grandpa left him some. He was getting liquor somehow.

"That's enough of that," I said out loud to myself. "I'm my own man. So is my dad. I'm going to take care of myself now. Him too, since he can't seem to do anything good for himself." I always wondered how he got the way he was. My grandpa raised him as well as he could, but somehow my dad fell in a well he couldn't drink himself out of. Now he's living with me. It was all upside down to me.

I made it look to my dad like I was going to school, but I had no intention of going to school. I walked downtown to my grandpa's, now, my lawyer's office like the insurance man told me to do. I enjoyed walking in the fresh air. It was about a mile from my house to downtown Yakima. There were lots of people driving around. I took my time. Even so, the office wasn't open when I got there so I went for a fast food breakfast sandwich thing which I hardly ever ate, as well as a cup of coffee. The girl behind the counter who sold it to me was pretty. She was young too, around my age, a little older maybe. I liked her a lot more than Laura, but having seen Laura naked let me imagine way better how that girl must look naked.

I was embarrassed by the time she said how much money I owed for my food. I got tongue tied so I stopped trying to talk. I gave her the money without looking up at her. I took my change as I tried to smile at her. To my surprise she was flashing me a big grin. All of a sudden she blinked both eyes at me. I felt like she had just taken my picture with her eyes. I grinned back at her as I stepped aside to get out of the way of the people behind me.

I sat at what looked like a clean table in a spot where I could see her doing her job. I noticed how she glanced over at me a couple of times. I ate kind of slow so I could see more of what she was like. Her hair was real black. She seemed nice enough to all the customers, but I didn't see her grin at anybody else. I decided I would come back to talk to her after I went to my lawyer and had taken care of my money.

I walked over to the lawyer's offices again. I sat outside their building on a wooden bench with four green painted slats for the seat and back which had lots of carving in it. I wanted to finish my coffee so I sat and watched people for a while. Most everybody I saw seemed pretty busy, like they had things to do. Men dressed in suits walked by, some had a briefcase or leather satchel of some kind. Women were dressed well in various types of blouses, skirts or slacks. I thought of my dad at home on the couch. Since he came home he had been wearing the same clothes he had on when I found him lurking around the back door of my house, except for when he was naked having sex. He was probably about the same age as quite a few of the men I saw walking around downtown.

That's the way it had gotten to be with me and my dad. I couldn't get him off my mind. I couldn't help wondering what if this? What if that? What if he had done some things differently? What if he had done everything differently? What if he was different? I always ended up with the same answer. No matter what he was like I only had him as my dad. I never had a choice in the matter. I know nobody can choose their own parents, their own family. But, if things had been different than they are right now I wouldn't be walking into a lawyer's office to figure out what to do with a bunch of money. I was rich. Would I have been rich if my real dad had raised me? Maybe I would be drinking right along with him. Wouldn't that be something?

I walked over to the trash barrel to throw my coffee cup away. As I went through the right side of the double swinging glass doors painted with the name of the law firm in three inch tall white and gold letters two men came out of the left side brushing against me. The men smelled of some sweet cologne that made me sneeze. I sat down in a chair next to a table covered in magazines that also had a nice big box of Kleenex. As I was blowing my nose a woman who looked like she was a model from a magazine approached me. She asked me if I needed help.

"Are you all right? Can I help you?" she said.

I nodded.

"Are you lost?"

"No I'm not lost. I'm here to see my lawyer."

"You are here to see a lawyer?"

"Yes."

"Do you have an appointment?"

"No I kind of have, well not an emergency, but I need to see my lawyer for some help with something."

"With no appointment. So what is your name and who is it that you want to see?"

"My name is Daryl Brown. My grandpa Bertrand Brown got me set up with Mr. Cartwright. I need to see Mr. Cartwright."

"Well I'm afraid Mr. Cartwright is a very busy man. Without an appointment you won't be able to see him today."

"Please can you tell him I'm here about some money problems I have since my grandpa died?"

She looked at me kind of funny. Like she didn't believe me.

"Daryl Brown, you said?"

"Yes, please can you tell him I'm here?"

"Have a seat. I'll have to let you know."

She left me sitting in the little room lined with soft puffy chairs. I stopped sneezing from the smell of the cologne. There was a nice aquarium opposite me with a few black and white angel fish in it. There were other fish but I didn't know their names. There was a long skinny looking fish with a sucker mouth stuck to the inside of the glass. I was the only one sitting there. The place smelled moist like water, but clean. I threw my dirty tissue in a small green plastic garbage can under the table.

There was a painting hanging on the wall above the aquarium of a barefoot bald man wearing a full length black coat. The man was holding a large black umbrella over his head while he was standing up on the seat in a small white boat. It looked like there was a big rainstorm on the lake. He was the only one in the little white boat. When I was looking at the man in the boat with the umbrella I imagined him swimming in what looked like would be very cold dark water when all of a sudden I heard a very deep voice calling my name.

"Daryl, I'm so glad to see you," the man said as he stretched out his hand for me to shake. "Your grandfather was such a great man. Come on in to my office so we can talk about what's on your mind."

I smiled as I shook Mr. Cartwright's hand. "Oh, yeah, I remember you now. You came to grandpa's funeral. I kind of forgot I met you before."

"Yes, your grandfather never brought you to my office. He did say a lot of wonderful things about you. He really loved you."

As Mr. Cartwright escorted me through a big wooden door past the woman who had come out from behind her glass reception counter to see what I wanted, she looked at me, smiled then she sat back down at her desk.

"You met Lydia already, on your way in didn't you?"

I nodded at him. He was whisking me right into his office. I got the impression Lydia was surprised.

I gave Lydia a little wave, "Hello Lydia, thanks for your help," I said.

She smiled at me again, with a real big smile this time.

Mr. Cartwright was shorter than me. Lots of people are. He was about five-feet, six-inches tall. His hands were pretty soft. He had white straight hair combed back real smooth. He smelled pretty good, kind of like Old Spice, like grandpa. Nothing like those two other guys who made me sneeze. Mr. Cartwright kept talking to me all the time as we walked into his comfortable but not big office. He told me where to sit. I sat down in a nice wooden chair with a straight back right in front of his desk. It felt good to sit up straight. He went behind his desk so we sat directly opposite each other. His office was nice, but not fancy. I tried to listen to everything he was saying, but I missed a lot of what he was talking about. It was mostly stuff about how he would go listen to my grandpa play his guitar sometimes. He said something about a band, some night clubs. I was pretty preoccupied with what I wanted to talk about. Then he asked me.

"So what's on your mind Daryl?"

I took a big deep breath.

"It's okay to breathe. Take a few more deep breaths if you need to. I'm here to help you."

"I know, thanks. I have a lot of things to think about and take care of since grandpa died. What I came in for today is this." I said as I pulled the cashier's check out of my other papers so I could slide it across his desk to him.

He put his half-type glasses on, looked at the check then looked at me over the top of his glasses. He smiled a very pleasant smile at me.

"You're grandpa has never stopped surprising me Daryl. He surprised me by dying. He and I are, or, I should say were the same age. Even though he has passed on he has surprised me with this too. I am very glad you came in to see me today. That was a good idea."

"Thanks, yeah the guy who brought it to me said to see a lawyer, or someone I trust."

"Well I hope you think you can trust me."

"Oh, yeah, I didn't mean that like it might have sounded" I said.

"Don't worry. I know I can help you with this windfall."

"I'm so glad I have someone to talk to about this. I really miss my grandpa. He did so much for me I don't know how to begin to thank him."

"Daryl, the best thing you can do for your grandfather is to live a good life."

"Do you mean not like my real dad?"

"What do you know about your real dad Daryl?"

"Well, I know he's living with me now?"

"Seriously?"

"Yeah, I wouldn't joke about a thing like that. He came by about a week after grandpa died. He was sitting on the back porch when I came home from school one day. He told me he was moving in with me to be my dad."

Mr. Cartwright sat silent while he rubbed his chin with the index finger and thumb of his right hand. After a few moments that seemed like minutes he spoke.

"Daryl, I don't like that your dad has come to live with you. I have had talks about him with your grandfather over the years. Your grandfather has tried desperately to keep you safe from what he, and I too, regard as a serious threat to your well-being."

"You think he's going to kill me?"

"No, no, no, nothing like that. But as long as your dad continues to abuse alcohol and drugs he will be a negative influence on you."

For the first time I felt angry for my dad. I mean who was this guy to try to keep me from knowing my own father.

"So you don't want me to get to know my own dad?"

"Daryl, I'm sorry that sounds very harsh. That isn't what I or your grandfather meant at all."

"So what did you mean?" I said.

"I don't mean any disrespect to you or any members of your family. I only want the best for you. Your grandfather was not only a client of mine he was a real friend. I want you to know I can be a real friend to you too."

"Mister Cartwright the truth is I'm really confused. I know my dad is a train-wreck. He's also my train-wreck. I stayed home from school sick when I wasn't sick to see what he did all day. I wanted to know what was going on with him. He looks sick. He has a big belly, his arms are kind of skinny. He has a bad cough, sometimes, not all the time. I wanted to know how he paid for all the beer and liquor he drinks every day. All he did all day was couch surf, watch TV or talk on the phone. He talks down to me if he talks to me at all. Last night he had some woman in my house. They were having sex on the couch where my grandpa died. I thought my dad was going to have a heart attack having sex with her. When she got off my dad she saw me watching them from the hallway then showed off her big naked boobs to me. She talked to me like I was a little kid. I'm emancipated. I'm a man. My dad thinks I'm some punk kid. He's my dad. I barely know him. He's a sick old drunk. I'm stuck with him."

Mister Cartwright listened to me almost as well as grandpa used to. I remembered back to what I said about my dad. I sounded ridiculous to myself. I looked up at the walls figuring that's why Mr.

Cartwright had such peaceful pictures in his office. He probably heard all kinds of stuff from all his clients.

He interrupted my thinking with his deep voice.

"Daryl," he said real solemn like. I figured he was going to give me a sermon or something.

"Daryl, I had a dad who drank too," he said.

I looked straight into his pale blue eyes. I'm sure he must have sensed my astonishment and relief.

"My dad was the kind of, beat-up-your-wife-and-if-your-kid-intervenes-knock-him-out, kind of drunk," he said. "I got beat up plenty defending my mom from my dad. I think it helped some, but after beating me up he still beat her up. I did get him tired out sometimes though, so he was too weak to do as much damage as he would have otherwise. Until the day I was late getting home from a football game on a Friday night when the cops were all over our house. My dad was being led out to a cop car when I got there. They wouldn't let me go in. I didn't get to see my mom until her funeral. He had beaten her to death while I was playing football for my high school team. Your grandpa transferred to my school about a week after that. We became friends. He was my age. He helped me grow up because he was the most loyal friend I have ever had. If it hadn't been for him I don't know what would have become of me. Your great-grandfather was also a drinker. Your grandpa knew what I was going through and he helped me. He was very good to me. We always helped each other for the rest of our lives. I never charged him a nickel for any legal work. I'm not going to charge you. I'm going to help you the best I can. I hope you understand what your grandfather and I mean when we say we don't want you to follow in your father's footsteps. We don't want you to go down the road of alcohol and drug abuse. That's one of the reasons why your grandfather has done so much for you. I hope telling you all this will help you trust me so I can help you."

I had listened intently to what Mr. Cartwright had told me. I took a few deep breaths, gave out a couple big sighs.

"I do trust you Mr. Cartwright. I trusted you before I came in here today because my grandpa trusted you. After what you told me today I know why my grandpa trusted you so much. Thanks for telling me all that. I didn't know about you and him. I mean I knew you have been his lawyer and everything, but, I didn't know the rest."

"So shall we move forward together? Anytime you need something you can call me okay."

"Okay," I said then I gave him a big grin. "So what should I do with this fortune grandpa left me?"

"Well the first thing we do is make sure it's secure in a place where only you can get access to it. That's easy enough. I have to tell you something you might not like Daryl."

"What?"

"You aren't really an emancipated individual. You are still too young. You need to be sixteen. I imagine you are disappointed about that, but don't worry about it. I'm going to make sure you're situation stays the same. Did you tell your dad about being emancipated?"

"Yeah, I told him."

"That's okay. Legally your grandfather took care of that anyway. You are, until you want to be emancipated at sixteen, under my legal guardianship. We already took care to make sure you were protected in the event that your dad did happen to show up at some time. Frankly I'm surprised he showed up at all. I guess your grandpa knew his son pretty well after all."

"Grandpa knew a lot about a lot of things."

"He sure did."

"So here's the thing. For today I want you to relax. Be assured everything is going to be all right with you. I don't know about your dad. What do you want to do with him?"

"Do with him?"

"Do you want to let him stay in your house?"

"He's my dad, even though he is messed up I can't throw him out."

"Okay. Do you feel in danger in anyway?"

"No. I think he's really sick. There's no way he can hurt me. I mean I could beat him up easy."

"Well don't do that. Don't let things get to the point where you want to do that either."

"I won't. I promise. The thing is I have the feeling that he came back home to be home. I know that sounds weird. Grandpa never wanted him to come home as long as he was drinking. So he stayed away. Then when grandpa died he came home. I think he wants a place to feel secure. I don't think he wants to go anywhere. I almost feel like he came home to die someplace besides the street, or some shelter."

"You're probably right Daryl. I'm no psychologist so I can't give you a professional opinion. What I can tell you is you're right. He is still you're dad. You have every right to love him even though he may not be nice to you. I bet he is jealous of the relationship you had with his father. He probably would have wanted the same kind of relationship with his dad that you had. Who wouldn't have? So as long as you feel safe living with him and want to get to know him I can't see any reason why you shouldn't."

"Thanks. Maybe I can even help him somehow."

"You are already helping him Daryl. You're allowing him to live with you, getting to know him. If it wasn't for you he would be homeless or worse. Using his wits for places to stay at night. As long as you feel safe, that's the main thing. Does he want you to drink with him?"

"I feel safe. I'm not scared of him or anything like that. And, no he doesn't ask me to drink with him."

"Okay then. If he ever wants you to start drinking with him, you call me. Okay? I'll find a safe place to invest the money you brought me today as well as keeping you notified of how things are going with it. I know I don't have to tell you this, but it makes me feel better to say it. No matter how much money your grandfather left you it will never be able to replace him in your life."

"That's for sure. But, now I've got my dad with me."

We stood up and shook hands. I left Mr. Cartwright's office feeling good. Then when I got outside, like had been happening recently, I started crying. The tears came in a wave of emotion. I sat down on an empty green bus bench while I cried for a couple of minutes until I could catch my breath.

As I looked down at the grey cement sidewalk I could see a small bird hopping around looking for food. I couldn't help but smile. It seemed so small, so out of place walking around on concrete with legs and feet designed for walking around in a forest or holding onto little branches in some tree. I hoped it had a nest in some tree in the downtown part of town. It didn't seem right for that little bird to have to live in a place made for cars, busses, and people. I couldn't help thinking maybe that's how my dad felt. I know I felt alone a lot of the time. Maybe my dad needed someone to give him food and drink that he liked so he could live someplace where he wasn't all alone. I felt like that too sometimes. If it hadn't been for my grandfather taking me in I would have been like one of those tiny dead birds you see drying up on the ground after they were pushed out of their parent's nest. A little shriveled up thing slowly eaten up by ants, or other bugs, maybe even a scavenger bird. Is that how my dad felt? Like me?

The bird flitted around then flew off. I looked up, dried my eyes, and then slowly made my way home. It was a warm day, a little too warm I thought. When I got to my gate I could see Maximus was lying on the grass not far from the front door. I called him, but he didn't move. I swung open the gate so I could run to him. I knelt down on the grass next to Maximus. He was chained up to some metal triangle looking thing stuck in the ground. I found the chain was attached to the triangle shaped top of a big metal screw that had been screwed into the ground about a foot. When I unchained him and took the screw out of the ground I could see there was no swivel or anything to let Maximus walk around. So when he did walk around he ended up choking himself. He was panting fast. From the looks of him he must have walked around and around the chain holder until he got it wound so tight he had to lay down. His eyes were closed. I looked around to see he had no food or water. I called his name again. He opened his eyes once then closed them. He looked real sick. I went in the house to get him some cold water. As I did so I could see my dad was snoring loudly as he lay on the floor next to the couch.

By the time I got back out to see Maximus he was breathing slower. I tried to get him to drink some cold water. I opened the left side of his mouth to pour a little water in between his teeth. He barely moved his tongue. I started crying again. Not so much as I did when I was downtown, but enough for some tears to fall onto Maximus's face.

I didn't think he was going to make it. So I quietly asked him, "So you want to be with Grandpa too huh?"

He was old, like Grandpa, but he had been tied up and ignored. My dad left him to die while he slept in the house. I sat on the grass next to Maximus for quite a while. He died right after sunset that day. He breathed slower and slower until there was no more breathing at all. Then I waited a while to go in the house to get as big a blanket as I could find. My dad was still out cold. I took a big old yellow blanket with frayed nylon borders from the linen closet. I slowly laid it out flat near his back. I grabbed his front legs and head so I could roll him onto the blanket. His back legs sort of came along in a twisted kind of way till they flopped over too. With his legs pointed into the center of the blanket I could roll up the rest of the blanket so he was all covered like a burrito. I tucked in the bottom of the blanket then I pulled him around the side of the house into the back yard. He had been losing weight or something because he seemed lighter than I thought he would be. I put a big garbage can on its side so I could slide him in. It was easier than I thought it would be. I put the lid on tight then went back around the front of the house to see if everything was okay before I went in. I took in the empty food and water bowl I wouldn't be using for Maximus anymore.

When I went in I saw my dad still sleeping. I took the bowls into the kitchen to set them in the sink. Then I went into my bedroom. Only when I lay down to look up at the ceiling did I remember I forgot to go back to the fast food place to talk to the pretty girl. My ceiling was dark when I turned off the light. I didn't want to see anymore that day.

I was so tired. I wanted to go to sleep, but I couldn't help hearing my dad snore. He had slept through the death of Maximus. My dad had killed my dog by tying him up in such a way that he would end up killing himself. Sounded to me like what happens to some people. They get all tied up by something they can't let go of until it kills them.

I felt like beating up my dad. There he was snoring like a log. I thought about getting out of bed, so I could go out to the living room to chain him to the floor so he couldn't go anywhere. He would have to stay in that one spot till he died. Then I would have to put him in a garbage can like Maximus. He already smelled like a dumpster. Maybe he would feel more at home there. No I don't think he could feel any more at home than he did on my grandpa's old couch or floor. My dad seemed perfectly content.

The only thing is I knew he was really sick. He was a drunk. His belly was all swelled up. Maybe he had lung cancer. No matter what was wrong with him he was still my dad. He had turned into my new Maximus. I was going to have to feed and water him until he died. Except his food was I don't know what and his water was some kind of booze, or beer. Yeah, my dad had turned into my helpless dog. He had backed himself into a corner he couldn't or wouldn't get out of. He was drinking himself to death.

My grandpa and Mr. Cartwright were both right about not drinking. I swore I would never drink alcohol. The thing is though, they were both wrong about me not being with my dad. They didn't want me to see him, be around him, or raised by him. Except I guess Mr. Cartwright was sort of right now. He trusted me to take care of my dad. That was good. If my dad hadn't come to live with me I would have always wondered what it would have been like to get to know him. Now I know I wouldn't have traded that knowledge for the world. I know why grandpa wanted to raise me. I'm so glad he did. I hate to think what would have happened to me if I had lived with my dad or my mom when I was little.

So once again I was staring at my bumpy ceiling thinking about my life. What would my life be like if that girl from the fast food place was my girlfriend? Tomorrow I would have to find out more about her. She had grinned at me. Right after I buried Maximus in the morning I would go to see her. My room was dark. The snoring quieted down. Dad must have rolled over.

The End

BROTHER LOUIS

Tulip trees blooming in the spring sunshine have grown into maturity since Brother Louis, C.S.C., a Holy Cross Brother first came to "the bluff". He enjoyed all the various trees, roses, azaleas, rhododendrons, camellias, as well as other flowers and shrubs he had a hand in growing. If anyone asked him if he had favorite plants he always said it was the ones with the most fragrant blossoms. In 1931 he had come to live at what some called "The Notre Dame of the West", the University of Portland, which gained "the bluff" nickname due to its location atop Waud's Bluff on North Willamette Boulevard in North Portland, Oregon. The university sits about 150 feet above the Willamette River atop Waud's bluff. The bluff was named after an Englishman Captain John Waud who came to Oregon in the 1850's. Looking south and down from the top of the bluff you can see Swan Island. Looking up and farther toward the south allows a view toward central Portland. The Willamette River which flows northwest out of central Oregon divides Portland "The City of Roses", from east to west then merges with the Columbia River at Kelley Point Park, to finish its flow to the Pacific.

Brother Louis came to Portland from South Bend, Indiana, via Chicago in June of 1931 traveling on Union Pacific's "Portland Rose", pulled by a massive 4-6-6-4 Challenger steam locomotive. By the time he arrived at what was at the time still called Columbia University, Swan Island was no longer an island. It was the site of Portland's municipal airport and remained so until 1940 when the airport was moved to its present location in the Northeastern part of the city off 82nd avenue. The east channel of the Willamette River, which the Army Corps of Engineers had wanted to close in 1876, was still open until 1927 when permission was obtained to change Swan Island into a peninsula.

When Brother Louis arrived in the summer of 1931 the university as well as the city of Portland were both quiet peaceful places. He arrived before the decade of huge changes that came to Portland in the pre-war and war years between 1935 and 1945. He was there to see things become very different.

Swan Island on the east side of the river had been reclaimed from the swamp land it had been next to the river to be transformed into farm land, then an airport, to eventually become what it remains today. Which is now an industrial area located below and a few hundred yards southeast of the University campus.

Brother Louis often sat on the grass or on the black cast iron legged bench with the much carved-in wooden slats that was about twenty feet east of the muzzle-plugged World War II cannon aimed directly south over Swan Island at downtown Portland. If it was raining or the grass was wet he stood, to keep as dry as he could. He enjoyed seeing various ships including naval vessels come and go from the dry dock at Swan Island. Naval ships often docked near Swan Island as well as making their annual visits docking near downtown for the Rose Festival the city of Portland sponsored every summer on the banks of the Willamette.

From his vantage point atop the high bluff he could see most of the city, not in detail, but with binoculars he could see parts of most of the bridges that connect east and west Portland. The first one in the line of bridges, which happens to be the most recently built, is The Fremont Bridge which looms high above the Willamette. The giant American Flag that flies atop the newest bridge to connect east and west Portland is easily discernible from the top of the bluff with the naked eye.

Brother Louis watched thousands of people cross The Fremont Bridge on people's day in 1973 when the bridge was new. With binoculars he could see, with an obstructed view, parts of the Broadway, Steel, Burnside, Morrison, and Hawthorne bridges pretty easily; however, the other bridges Marquam, Ross Island and Sellwood, south of the Hawthorne Bridge were obscured from his vantage point. The bridges north of the University, St. John's Bridge and the principal railroad bridge, he couldn't see at all. And even though it wasn't possible for him to see it from his viewpoint near the cannon, he was familiar with Cathedral Park under the St. John's Bridge; because, he had visited there long before it became an attractive spot for students from the university to enjoy recreational activities.

Brother Louis loved being able to sit and watch the city. At a distance he could see how things changed. For him even though it was easier to pick out details by using them, he preferred to look at the city without binoculars. He used to say that using binoculars gave things a false perspective. But, it wasn't the city alone he was concerned with. He thought about and prayed for many things going on the world.

While he spent time looking out over the top edge of Waud's bluff at the city, he also had a commanding view across the wide Willamette river valley toward the southern hills that loom over the river as it exits the city of Portland. Many times over the years he witnessed storms coming at him from that direction. He could see treetops on the hills across the valley bend and wave like grass as the wind blew hard and fast. He would wait for a storm to span the valley as it worked its way up the face of the bluff. He smiled as the wind got stronger and stronger, ruffling his clothing, threatening his hat. The storms could cool him so much he sometimes had to go inside. Along with the times when it would rain on part of the campus while the sun shone brightly on another part, watching storms come in was one of those routine weather occurrences, common in Portland, he never tired of during all his years at the university.

In January of 1975 he had been at the university for nearly forty-five years. He had celebrated various anniversaries. His own as well as those of his congregation's brothers. For the most part Louis devoted his work time as a religious brother to his responsibility for the landscaping at the "Notre Dame" of the west. He knew the grounds better than anyone else. Some of the trees were original to the land on which the university was built; however, many were planted under his direction. He always wondered who had planted the trees that were there before he came to the campus.

For him not knowing who planted the trees on campus was like no one knowing exactly when Swan Island started being called Swan Island. At some time it just became Swan Island. Which reminded him of the way Fr. Ignatius his confessor friend's nephew got one of his names. Sammy's given name was Marshall. A day or two after Marshall was born, Marshall's grandfather Owen started calling him Sammy. Everybody in the family knew Grandpa Owen was very forgetful, so teasing Marshall by calling him Sammy was an inside the family joke. What happened was that for a few days after Marshall was born Grandpa Owen kept calling baby Marshall Sammy. In the excitement and confusion of having a new baby with a new name some of the family members also started calling Marshall Sammy. Many in the family thought Marshall's name was Sammy; because, they heard him being called Sammy more often, mostly by Grandpa Owen than anyone else, that, they thought Sammy was at least part of Marshall's given name, which it isn't. It was kind of confusing. Marshall was twelve years old when Brother Louis met him. When they were introduced Marshall told Brother Louis his name was Marshall and he preferred being called Marshall. So Brother Louis always called Marshall by his given name and never Sammy. Brother Louis's friend Fr. Ignatius told Louis he enjoyed the confusion in his family. But, that kind of familiarity between the two men developed quite some time after they had come to know and love each other.

Brother Louis was appointed head landscaper at the University of Portland within a few years of his arrival. During his forays around campus his head was often pointed toward the ground to search out unwanted pests of all kinds. He also scanned the trees and bushes to see if they were in need of special attention. His well worked hands and the permanent tan on the back of his leathered neck gave away some of the secrets as to what he did. In a restaurant or bus, even at a university event he could have easily been mistaken for an old ranch hand from Eastern Oregon who came to town to check on his daughter's progress in the nursing program, or his son's success in the school of engineering. The very things that University of Portland parents did to see if they were getting their money's worth. Brother Louis also spent a lot of time looking up at the sky when he was outside. The weather in Portland can change quickly. He enjoyed watching clouds form, then reform, only to drop their moisture and move on.

After forty-five years on "the bluff", Brother Louis was starting to show his age. In his time at the school he had grown older, balder, even, a bit plump. When he was working he usually wore a Portland Pilot's baseball cap that helped to keep out the intermittent rain, known locally as Portland sunshine, from his eyes that occurred during a good portion of the school year. For summer work he changed out the cap for a plastic green visor which he wore to honor his late mother's memory. She always wore a plastic green visor when she gardened. So that's why he did.

For years he often pushed his wooden-handled wheelbarrow with the pneumatic tire a bit underinflated. More than once the tire got so bad it had to be replaced. Eventually one of his student helpers got one of those airless hard rubber ones to replace it thinking it would be an improvement; however, Louis missed the slight bounce of the air filled tire. It gave a bit more cushion going over obstacles or curbs. When he pushed it with the air tire it seemed to float softly on the grass. The hard rubber tire made a deeper dent in the grass, tools in the wheelbarrow bounced harder making more noise.

He always had a rake, shovel or both in his wheelbarrow. He always needed one or the other as he was going around. He had helpers working under his supervision, paid professionals that worked for the university, as well as student workers. He always reminded everyone who worked with him if something went wrong it was his responsibility. He was where the buck stopped. So he always told his workers they must be careful to keep him out of hot water with the university president. That tactic seemed to work well for him.

That tactic worked because everybody who ever came into contact with Brother Louis, whether they worked with him or not, could tell he was a holy man. If they didn't know what holy meant before they met him they began to understand what it meant to be a holy person by being around him. People would say things like: "You know that Brother Louis is kind of different, kind of, I don't quite know how to explain it. He seems different than a lot of people, like holy or something, like he's got some kind of "in", with God." The more they got to know him the more they became convinced of his holiness.

Brother Louis read a few books, mostly about world history, seldom went to movies. He went to restaurants only when his friends could convince him to go. He spent most of his waking time outdoors or in church. He rose early in the morning to spend time praying in silence and solitude before most of the rest of the world around him woke up.

Brother Louis was not a learned man. He joined the Confraternity of the Holy Cross to become a brother. He didn't consider himself priestly material. Even though he read some of the newspapers he came across in the community lounge there were only a few books besides the bible he enjoyed reading, and most of those were concerned with prayer.

He loved being outdoors. He loved nature, plants, animals and people. He grew up on a farm in rural Indiana. His mom lost the farm when Louis's father died. She moved herself and Louis to South Bend, Indiana, where she thought Louis, her only child, might one day be able to attend Notre Dame. He made her very happy when he decided to enter religious life. She was delighted to know he was going to be a member of the C.S.C, the Congregation of the Holy Cross, the religious order that runs Notre Dame. Knowing that her son loved everyone and everything around him she thought surely he would prosper in a place where he could do what he did best, finding the good in everybody.

Brother Louis's mom passed away a year after he entered religious life. Two years later he volunteered to head west to help in the ongoing development of what had started as Columbia University in Portland, Oregon. The grounds had changed hands a few times before it became a property of his congregation and Brother Louis arrived in Portland before, in 1935, the school had changed its name from Columbia University to the University of Portland.

During his years at the university he inspired more than one profligate student worker paying off their debt to the university to want to be more than a pansy planter. By his example and kindness he helped both men and women students to believe in themselves enough to make the most of their personal gifts and talents. Brother Louis would tell his workers to do a good job so he wouldn't get into trouble with the president of the university. No one who ever worked with Brother Louis wanted to get him in trouble with the president of the university. Brother Louis was a man from whom goodness flowed. Everybody knew it, because they could feel it.

Eventually, Brother Louis's friend Fr. Ignatius became especially aware of Brother Louis's condition. Fr. Ignatius taught theology. He had taught theology at more than one university. He had even taught theology at Notre Dame. Brother Louis knew how important Fr. Ignatius was to the University of Portland and the Congregation of the Holy Cross. Fr. Ignatius had been told by members of his congregation, that Brother Louis was the kind of person who had come to represent the heart and soul of the University of Portland. And in addition many of his confreres thought Brother Louis represented what was best and most important to the Congregation of the Holy Cross. Fr. Ignatius eventually became more than Brother Louis's friend. He became Louis's confessor. Which meant that not only did Br. Louis confess his sins to Fr. Ignatius, Louis also let Fr. Ignatius guide his soul. A task he had entrusted to his previous confessor of many years, Fr. Byron C.S.C., who had died of cancer in 1973.

Guiding a soul is a rarefied task. There is truly nothing more sublime than advising a person on how to live in such a way that they are in fact not only staying out of trouble as far as sinning goes. There is the priceless guidance that a person's confessor gives to a person that helps them live up to their God given potential. It is a confessor's task and responsibility to help a person be the most loving person they can be, as well as deepening their relationship with God in all aspects of their life.

When Brother Louis first came out west he had to find a new confessor; because, the one he had during his formative years as a brother stayed in South Bend. Louis did his best to land someone with whom he felt comfortable. It took him a while to find someone he trusted. Fr. Byron had fulfilled that role a long time. Brother Louis missed having someone help him discern his life. He needed a new confessor to confide in. Brother Louis had been taught that having a spiritual confessor would help keep him on the right path. He had seen enough people in religious life leave their congregations. He wanted to fulfill the commitment he had made to God for his whole life.

Brother Louis knew his relationship with God was like gardening. If a gardener wanted a plant to thrive it was necessary to put in the necessary nurturing criteria for the best results. Everything had to be just right: the soil, the water, the amount of light, the right fertilizer. There were a lot of things that had to be taken into consideration for plants to thrive. There were so many kinds of plants with so many different needs. Brother Louis knew people are like plants.

Which is why he always availed himself of the grace he received from participating in the sacrament of confession every Saturday afternoon. He never committed any grave or mortal sins. His offenses, if they could be called such, were always of the less than venial variety. What he considered his personal sins most people would have thought inconsequential to themselves or anyone else. He rarely did anything that anyone else would consider wrong. But, after many years of personal struggle Brother Louis had developed a very refined sense of right and wrong. He knew everything he did had consequences for someone else, so he did not want to do wrong things. For example, Brother Louis would never drink coffee; because, he knew many of the people who grew and picked the beans for coffee were being severely underpaid for their product. He did not want to be part of that injustice.

Brother Louis wanted a confessor who could help him keep doing right things. He relied on the seal of confession for being able to voice his gravest concerns about the state of his soul with his confessor without fear of anyone else ever knowing. The only people besides himself and God who ever knew what Brother Louis spoke most deeply about himself and many other things had been his two confessors. When he heard that Fr. Ignatius, a learned theologian with a good reputation was coming to the university, he wanted to see perhaps, if the man had time, the two of them might consider discussing the possibility of Fr. Ignatius becoming Brother Louis's spiritual confessor. Brother Louis wanted someone to help him be as good a person as he could be.

Fr. Ignatius was a tall man. He stood six foot four on his bare feet. His posture was arrow straight. If not for his graying wavy hair he could have passed for a Portland Pilot athlete. Along with his straight arrow posture he was strong, sinewy. He had learned when he was young, when he did play basketball for Notre Dame, and before he joined the Congregation of the Holy Cross, the wisdom of weight lifting exercises. He continued to lift weights his whole life, not for bulk, but for toning. When he was in college he had been approached by more than one ad agency offering him the possibility of becoming a model. He politely declined those offers, not because he wasn't flattered, but because he had been considering a religious vocation since he was a child. He had thought about becoming a priest in the Catholic Church since he was in first grade.

Having gone to Catholic grade school and high school he had ample time to observe a variety of priests. Some of them were very inspiring to him. During his college years he spent plenty of time with friends both male and female to be able to know what he would be missing if he decided to be a celibate priest who would never marry. He seriously considered the possibility of marriage. The young Ignatius gave a lot of thought to the many options open to him. He was smart, kind, considerate, reflective. There were more than a few young women very interested in him, which gave some of his male friends a few twinges of jealousy. Even so everybody he knew liked him. His sincere winning personality, intelligence, and good looks made him popular.

Brother Louis knew of Fr. Ignatius by reputation before he met him. Fr. Ignatius came out to "the bluff" for a few visits before moving there to teach theology at the University. As he was wont to do Brother Louis kept his attendance at community soirees limited to an hour or less per event. So the first time the two men were introduced was at a regularly scheduled Friday night dinner get-together in the community dining room. Fr. Ignatius, who was still a visiting guest, sat near the end of the head table. He was wearing his clerics, black shirt with the white collar indicative of his priestly vocation along with the requisite black pants and shoes.

Brother Louis was dressed in his usual outfit, long sleeve button-up grey work shirt. His brown work pants cinched up with one of the two black belts he owned, that, if he took off and held up to let hang, would be quite curved for they had both conformed to his shape. Brother Louis sat at one of the tables in a line off to the left of the head table. The thirty or so members of the congregation present sat along the outside of the row of tables so all the men could see each other.

Community dinners always started with a prayer of thanksgiving for their meal after which the senior congregation official would stand to introduce any visitors to the gathered brothers. He would introduce them, ask them to stand, say a few words if they so desired, after which time the meal would commence. When Fr. Ignatius was introduced Brother Louis smiled at him. Fr. Ignatius saw, like everybody else did who was blessed by a smile from Brother Louis, something that seemed different about the old brother sitting at a table of religious men. Fr. Ignatius smiled back then sat down. When he did so he could not help glancing over at Louis throughout that meal. Brother Louis tried to meet with Fr. Ignatius at the dinner, but the popular priest was engaged in conversation with members of the theology department and the president of the university. Brother Louis left the dinner after about an hour thinking if it was meant to be he would have a chance to visit with Fr. Ignatius.

Fr. Ignatius had done a little asking around before changing communities. People in religious life change communities or assignments for a lot of noble reasons, as well as some less than noble reasons. It was a big move, perhaps seen by some as a step down or demotion to move from Notre Dame, to "the bluff". Much more prestige was attached to the University in South Bend than the one out in the northwest.

Portland during the seventies and before was considered by many to be not much more than an overgrown small town. It was one of those many cities that blossomed due to the war effort in the forties then decreased in size and importance once the war was over. Seattle, in Washington, which is a critical port in the western United States, as well as Portland in northern Oregon did not have nearly the status they would eventually claim. The Pacific Northwest simply did not have the prominence or public prestige of places in California or the Eastern and Southern parts of the United States. So for a well-respected theologian who was the author of more than one textbook used in colleges where he taught; there was some speculation as to why he might be moving to "the bluff". Fr. Ignatius had heard some of the rumors being floated around about him by members of his community as to why he was going to be in Portland. He tried his best to ignore what he considered murmuring.

At first, Fr. Ignatius came to Portland to teach for a year. He stipulated to his religious superior at Notre Dame, that if he so chose, he could come back to Notre Dame to his same position as full professor after a year. The agreement was made. Fr. Ignatius would come out to the University of Portland on the bluff to help inspire as well as to beef up, so to speak, the theology department which had long needed some help. Which created some tension in the theology professors who felt somewhat slighted by his arrival. He got to the university two weeks before the start of the academic year in the autumn of 1975, forty-four years after Brother Louis had come. Fr. Ignatius had just turned forty-two years old.

May first of 1975 Brother Louis celebrated his seventieth birthday. Ignatius was forty-two. Louis had lived through a few more wars than Ignatius. Had spent nearly forty-five years at a school where a new professor was going to see how things went. After their first community dinner together where Fr. Ignatius was formally introduced to his brethren the two men would have most likely rarely crossed paths on a regular basis. One was a groundskeeper, the other a highly respected professor with an international reputation as a theological scholar. If it hadn't been for the way the campus was designed their relationship may have disappeared altogether. If it hadn't been for the fact that Brother Louis had lost his long time confessor Fr. Byron to death by cancer he wouldn't have needed a new confessor. But he did need one, which is why he wanted to try out Fr. Ignatius.

It happened that one sunny day after the noon mass at St. Mary's chapel on the south side of campus, Brother Louis sat in one of his usual spots, on the bench near the cannon that faced downtown Portland. When he spotted Fr. Ignatius coming around the side of the chapel he smiled. It appeared as if Fr. Ignatius might be coming his direction.

Fr. Ignatius approached the general area of the cannon near where Brother Louis was sitting on the bench. Fr. Ignatius looked toward downtown Portland as he pointed at the Fremont Bridge. Then he said, "What is that high bridge with the big flag?"

"That's the Fremont Bridge. Peregrine falcons live there. It's named after John Fremont an Oregon explorer. It connects interstate 405 and US highway 30 to Interstate 5. It's a busy one," Brother Louis said. "I watched them lift up the bridge with hydraulic jacks a couple of years ago. At that time the "Guinness" book of records said it was the biggest hydraulic lift ever made. I don't know if it's still the biggest lift or not, but it's still there."

"Falcons live there?"

"Yeah. They help keep the bridge clean. The falcons eat quite a few of the pigeons that scavenge off the grain ships at the downtown docks. Otherwise there would be a lot more pigeons nesting on the bridge. Pigeons can do a lot of damage."

Fr. Ignatius laughed. "Yeah I suppose they would."

"That's kind of funny to you is it?"

"A bit ironic maybe, anyway, don't you think? The boats bait in the pigeons to feed the falcons."

"It's not a natural thing for any of them. There's too many pigeons because of all the grain near the river. There wouldn't be all that grain to be shipped out of here by the boatload if people weren't hungry all over the world. I've been near the docks. It smells like grain down there. Most of the ships are from foreign countries in need of food. All those pigeons eaten by the Peregrines wouldn't be there if it weren't for a human need being met by farmers sending all kinds of grain from their farms out east of here. In fact from all over the Northwest including Oregon, Washington, Idaho, Montana, and from wherever else the trains bring all that grain."

"Sounds like Portland is the Chicago of Oregon."

"That's about it. It's kind of like this campus. Sometimes I feel bad that all the plants and flowers on campus attract so many little birds that get killed and eaten by some wandering neighborhood cats."

"So you know a lot about Portland."

"I know the little bit I see from here, things I read about. Sometimes I get downtown. I mostly stay here minding my own business."

"Your business?"

"My business is being the best Holy Cross brother I can be."

"So how are you doing with that?"

Brother Louis leaned back into the bench, took a deep breath then leaned forward putting his hands together while he placed his forearms on the top of his thighs. He rubbed his hands together, meshed his fingers together back and forth then sighed. "I don't know, I can't tell by myself."

Fr. Ignatius had not expected this elderly man to make such a candid admission that may have seemed rather self-degrading, then he asked. "You can't tell?"

"Can you? You're a priest. Do you know if you're being a good priest?"

Brother Louis had asked the question everyone at some time or another asks about themselves no matter who they are, or what they do. Fr. Ignatius went into a zone of silence from which Brother Louis had emerged not long before.

After a few moments of looking out over Swan Island at the city of Portland Fr. Ignatius asked, "Mind if I sit with you a while?"

Brother Louis scooted from the middle of the bench over to his left. He sat with his knees wide apart, the bottom of his left thigh resting on the wood that was connected by carriage bolts to the one piece cast iron support structure that held the wood for the seat and back of the bench. Fr. Ignatius also sat with his knees apart, while his right leg rested on the wood connected by the carriage bolts to the wood support piece on the right side of the bench leaving about three feet of bench space between the two men. They could each feel the tops of the cold carriage bolts on the undersides of their thighs that secured the wood to the bench legs.

As they looked out over the river they sat in silence feeling whatever they could that came from the other man. They sat that way for a while. Each of them perceiving what the other was bit, by bit exuding.

After a few minutes Br. Louis asked. "Fr. Ignatius, I was wondering if you would consider being my confessor?"

"Are you asking me to hear your confession?"

"I don't mean confession right now. I need a confessor as a spiritual guide. I miss that. I had one for a while. Now I don't have one."

"Brother Louis, I've felt goodness coming from you. Like you are a person who is good. It comes out of you. I have never felt that from another human being. I think maybe you should be my confessor."

Brother Louis laughed out loud. "If you only knew my sins you would have a different opinion about me."

Gray clouds crossed in front of the midday sun. Brother Louis pointed over the valley to the wooded hills above the river. "See the trees moving?"

Fr. Ignatius nodded.

"This is one of my favorite things in the world. I sit here to watch the wind push the clouds over the valley. If we don't want to get wet we'll have to move in a few minutes. The wind is like a big wave of energy pulling along the clouds that drop all the beautiful rain which keeps us green here year round. We only have to wait until the storm arrives. You won't have to guess when we need to get inside. The wind blows through the valley over the river as it ripples waves into the water. Then the wind rushes up the cliff side of this bluff with enough force to blow off my hat. Most of the time after the wind gets to this spot, it takes a couple of minutes for the clouds to arrive. If we're still here when that happens we'll be getting wet. It usually gets colder and colder until the rain comes. Sometimes I wait to get rained on. Depending on how I feel, how much it rains, maybe I don't wait for the rain. Sometimes I go to my room."

"Today?"

"Today? I can't tell yet. I think maybe we should go to our rooms; because, that way you can think about what I asked you. You're new, I don't want the president of the university hearing I made his new professor sick by introducing him to what the weather of Portland can to do someone who just arrived."

Fr. Ignatius laughed, then said. "Okay. I'll do my thinking. But, let's wait here a little longer. I want to know what the weather here is really like."

When Brother Louis gazed west toward the wind he smiled, then said, "Here it comes."

As Fr. Ignatius watched Brother Louis peer into the wind, he found himself breathing out a deep sigh of relief that felt as if some heavy burden he hadn't known he was carrying flowed out with his breath to be carried away by the wind. While the two men awaited the fast moving storm looming at them from over the valley of the Willamette River, Fr. Ignatius quietly sobbed into the face of the storm. His hot tears mixed with the cool Portland rain pelting his cheeks. For the first time in his life, Fr. Ignatius felt real joy; because, he began to realize what he had wanted to find in religious life had found him.

The End

BUTOL OBLONSKI

A pair of men's powder blue boxer type underwear shorts hung on Butol Oblonski's office door. They were stained yellow on the front and smelled like dead fish. Butol found them on the way into his office where he worked in an advertising group with a staff of ten people. There were his bosses. The partners, Mr. Broom and Mr. Williams who were very pleased with Butol; because not only was Butol reliable, competent, and level headed. He had a knack for seeing into the feasibility of developing projects that were worth pursuing.

Butol was the immediate boss of two men who played practical jokes on him. Ray Kismet and Bert Janus, who were both hired about the same time. The two of them had a natural rapport between themselves. They were in their late twenties, had been with other firms, but their experience in developing marketing plans was limited so Butol guided them.

From the beginning of Ray's time with Broom and Williams he had played jokes on Butol. Butol laughed a little at some of the jokes because he was trying to encourage Ray to be comfortable in his new job. But, not everything Ray did was intended to prank

Butol. On his first day in the office Ray brought in a bouquet of Chrysanthemums. He had no idea that Butol was allergic to them. Butol's eyes swelled up, he sneezed and sneezed. Ray couldn't help but laugh. He had never known anyone who was allergic to Chrysanthemums. Bert watched Ray apologize to Butol.

Butol's reply was a simple "Oh, don't worry about it. How could you have known?"

When Bert and Ray were back in their office Bert leaned forward on his desk, propped up his head with his left hand as he quietly whispered to Ray, "That Butol must be a real wimp."

Ray got rid of the flowers into the trash, but it was Bert who kept them in mind.

It was the flowers that got Bert going on Butol. At the time not even Bert knew how inspirational those flowers had been. Together Ray and Bert played jokes on Butol; however, after a while Butol mostly ignored them. He didn't want to encourage their pranks. He thought it would be better for them to get bored so they would stop on their own.

During Butol's frequent lunches with his consultant friend Dick, Butol talked about many things, including Ray and Bert. Butol's friend Dick, whose full name, Richard Edward Millstone, was an IT consultant to Brown and Williams. Dick's offices were the whole floor above the offices of Brown and Williams. Where he, along with his very well paid and loyal employees worked on computer programming for various businesses. Dick was very intelligent as well as somewhat abrupt. He liked Butol very much, treated him like a younger brother. He felt sorry for Butol when Bert and Ray pulled pranks on him. Dick didn't know the Mums were the inspiration for the beginning of a string of pranks, including the latest one involving smelly underwear that Butol found when he came back to the office.

Butol and his wife Emily had been on vacation with their three children in Florida. They had flown from their home in Los Angeles to Orlando, Florida. On the way there the children took naps or played quietly during the mostly night flight. They returned to California on a day time flight.

"Mom, what's that down there?" Nonny asked as she leaned over her mother's lap to look out the window again.

"That's the Mississippi river delta," She told her.

Mrs. Emily Oblonski was a tall blond woman. Even now she looked as though she could have walked off the cover of a fashion magazine. She played tennis and swam to keep in shape after having had three children. She was a few years younger than her husband, had grown up in a family of fundamental Christians, but felt at ease with a more relaxed attitude about religion. She was very religious in her own way. She and Butol always took their children with them to church on Sundays. She kept her kids busy with school as well as extra-curricular activities to keep them on the straight and narrow. Emily didn't work at a job outside the house after she started having children. She made the decision to be a stay at home mom when she was pregnant with her first child Donny. Even though she was an accredited school teacher. Emily debated whether or not to home school her children and decided not to; because, she thought it was good for them to be in school with other kids.

The three Oblonski children were Donny, who at twelve was the oldest, Nonny two years younger and called Nonny, short for Nannette with two ns she told everyone. As a toddler she used to wander around the house saying Nonny, as she was trying to say Donny. The name stuck. She became Nonny. Mitchell was the baby. He was born during a storm. Butol had been afraid they weren't going to make it to the hospital on time. Mitchell waited to be born, in spite of delays due to traffic, until they got to the hospital. Then and still, Mitchell who's only seven going on eight is the most patient person in the family.

On the flight back from Miami to L.A. in daylight Nonny had a window seat and asked her mom about nearly everything she saw outside. The boys were more interested in thumb wrestling each other on the fold down tray and napping than trying to figure out what was on the ground. Butol read Kiplinger's, napped a little, then smiled and kissed his wife when he woke up.

While they were in Florida, they had stayed together for their various activities during most of the trip. They went to Disney World, Universal Studios, and Epcot Center together. Then on separate days, they split into two groups. The men went fishing or exploring while the ladies went their own way. The two boys wanted to see an alligator farm. Nonny did not. Mom and Nonny kept their activities secret from the boys. They didn't want to tell the boys about what they did, even when they got home. Which was more of Emily trying to make Nonny feel special and important than it was keeping secrets from her husband. Emily and Butol kept regular cell phone contact throughout the day while they were in Florida.

When Butol arrived at the office on the first Monday after he got back from Florida, he found a pair of underwear hanging on his office door. The powder blue boxer style underwear was hanging so the heavily stained front flap was in full view. The shorts were stained as if someone had gone to the bathroom in them multiple times, never washed them and let them dry. Butol gingerly picked them off the door knob with the thumb and forefinger of his left hand by gripping the elastic band. Then he addressed his secretary who he presumed was already inside the office.

"Hi Linda," He said so she could hear him on the other side of the door. He also knocked on the door with his right hand while he looked up and down the hall to see if anyone was around.

The door opened. Mr. Oblonski entered his outer office where his secretary worked.

"Mr. O. Why are you knocking?" she asked. "What is that?" she asked as she looked at the underwear Butol was holding.

"It's the reason we need to have the door handle sanitized," Butol said matter-of-factly. "It's someone's dirty underwear."

"What in the world?" she asked. "They sure stink," She said holding her nose.

Butol looked absently at the shorts in his hand. "I found them on our office door knob."

Linda shook her head. "On our entrance door?"

"Yeah it's a small gift to welcome me back to work."

"Oh Butol, that wasn't there when I came in and Dick, Mr. Millstone, is waiting for you in your office. He didn't mention seeing them when he came in," she explained.

"It's no big deal," Butol said. "I want to get rid of them with as little fanfare as possible. Have we got any extra garbage bags I can drop it in? Then I can take it to the trash."

"I'm sure we do," she said, as she began looking for a trash bag. "I hope we don't have to smell that all day."

"I know," Butol said. "Let's get rid of them ASAP. "They smell like dead fish right? Hey, I did go fishing while I was gone."

Linda crinkled her nose at him. "They stink!" She said as she produced a new garbage sack from the office supply closet. "I got a bag with a lemon smell that I hope takes care of that stench."

"I know," Butol said. "Pretty bad huh?"

"Here" she said as she opened the sack as wide as possible for Butol to drop the smelly shorts into the bag.

He gently lowered the dirty smelly underwear into the bag, released his grip on the elastic band to let them fall into the bottom of the bag. Then he took the bag from Linda, and tied it shut.

"I'll be back in a minute. I'm going to run down to the restroom and get rid of this. I need to wash my hands of it."

"Yeah," Linda said. "I'm so sorry Butol."

"Thanks."

"Do you think it was Bert and Ray?"

Butol shrugged, "I guess, who else? But, I really don't know. I really don't want to know. So let's forget about it okay?"

"Forget about it?"

"Yeah. Let's forget about it. Linda get Mr. Broom for me at his convenience will you?"

"Sure."

When Butol came back from the restroom he found the janitor washing the door to his office. The man looked up when he saw Butol coming.

"Good morning Mr. Oblonski," he said smiling. "I'm getting your door all cleaned up for you. Linda said it needed a bit of a cleanup. I didn't find anything real bad so I figured a good sanitizing with these pre-made sanitizer cloths would do the job."

"Thanks Harry," Butol said smiling back at Harry the janitor. "I really appreciate you getting it cleaned up so quickly. I've got some clients coming by this week. It's nice to have it all polished up. It makes a good impression."

"Happy to help out," Harry said as he opened the door wide for Butol to go in.

"Hi Linda," Butol said giving his secretary a big thumbs-up. "It's a done deal all the way around."

She smiled. "I did tell you Mr. Millstone is waiting for you, didn't I?"

"Yeah, thanks, you know how he is. I'm sure he's enjoying my office as his office-away-from-office, like a home-away-from-home, like he usually does. I think he would rather be in my office than his own. You'd think when you have your own floor with the best views you'd be content to stay there," Butol joked.

Linda laughed. "I understand. I have a sister who is the same way. She has a nicer house than me, but she's constantly coming to my house."

"Talk to you later. Oh yeah, thanks for keeping that door thing to yourself," he said.

She nodded.

Butol took a long deep breath as he entered his own inner office letting the door self-close behind him.

He took off his coat, hung it on the corner rack then opened the blinds to let in as much light as possible. He walked around the guest chair that faced his desk so he could sit down in his own chair behind the desk. Dick Millstone was sitting in one of Butol's guest chairs that he had placed next to Butol's chair, facing away from the desk toward the big window. Butol smiled at Dick, then moved the picture of his wife and kids away from the pile of papers on his desk so he could begin sorting through his mail. He found the post card he always sent himself when he was on a trip. Butol had gotten into the habit of buying and sending to himself at work a post card as soon as he arrived at his destination. On the card he would always write the same thing: "Having a great time. Wish you were still here."

Dick Millstone had been sitting in Butol's office waiting for Butol to come in. He had already looked to see what was in Butol's mail. Dick sat facing the window as he leaned back in one of Butol's swivel chairs. He had the back of the chair propped against Butol's desk like he usually did. Dick had actually gotten a foot rest installed on the wall near the window where he could put his feet so he could comfortably lean back in a chair at the same time. He held the back of his head in his hands while he gazed out the window.

Dick knew Bert and Ray would play some kind of prank on Butol while he was on vacation. Dick didn't know what though. They always did something to welcome Butol back to the office. Even when Butol went on a day conference they did something to him. Dick wondered why they did such childish things to a guy as nice as Butol. He was frustrated and felt powerless when Butol would confide in him about the tricks they did; because, even though Butol told him what they did, he never did anything about it, and didn't want Dick to do anything about it either. More than a few times, Dick had talked himself blue in the face trying to convince Butol to confront them. Dick went so far as to suggest he would take care of it once and for all for Butol. Dick told Butol more than once he would do whatever it took to stop Bert and Ray from pranking him. Whatever it would take, Dick told him, no one would ever know.

But, no, Butol told him the best thing was to ignore them, to let their pranks get old and boring to them. Butol tried to convince Dick they would stop on their own. So, Dick let Butol have his way, even though he strongly disagreed with him. Dick would have stopped those annoying pranks immediately. No questions asked. Bert and Ray would have stopped bothering Butol after the first time. There would have been no second prank if Butol had let Dick handle it.

"As usual only one good thing in the mail for me," Butol told Dick.

"Yeah," Dick agreed. "The best thing you get when you get back from vacation is your own card."

"So how long have you been waiting for me," Butol asked.

"About twenty minutes or so. I figured you would have quite a bit of mail for me to look at since you've been gone."

Butol smiled, then asked "Why don't you open it and read it for me?"

"Butol, I'm shocked, that's a federal offense. Of course I did read your postcard," Dick said.

"Like you care?"

Dick laughed. "I'm so glad you're back my friend. I missed you."

"I missed you too Dick," Butol said. "If you weren't here I would have called you about the underwear."

"Underwear? What are you talking about? You're not turning into some kind of pervert are you Butol?" Dick asked.

"There was a pair of dirty boxers hanging on the outside handle of my office door when I came in."

"I didn't see anything when I came in."

"I know, neither did Linda."

"You know who did it don't you Butol?"

"I've got a pretty good idea."

"What are you going to do?"

"I can handle them. It seems like ignoring their pranks works for a while; until, they come up with some new silly idea they think is funny. I'm not going to give any acknowledgement to them about the underwear thing though. When they don't get any reaction out of me they can think what they want. I do get tired of their games. At the same time I don't want to give them the satisfaction of letting them think their pranks bother me. They'll stop on their own."

"Yeah, well we both know their childish practical jokes do bother you. And obviously they haven't stopped yet," Dick said.

"Ah, heck with it. I've got so many more important things to think about than that. Speaking of which I'm trying to catch up with Mr. Broom sometime today," Butol explained trying to change the subject.

"Yeah, well," Dick began. "Speaking as your friend I think letting this go on isn't working to stop them. I know you've got things to do. I wanted to catch up with you too."

"Thanks Dick," Butol replied. "I appreciate that. I can handle those two guys. So don't worry about them okay?"

"Sure, I know you've got things to do so I'll go back upstairs. Let me know when you want to have lunch."

"You know I will."

Dick headed back to his offices on the floor above.

Butol began to sort through more of his mail. As he did so he began to think about what to do about Bert and Ray.

Bert and Ray shared an office and a secretary. They had desks together in the same room. They butted the fronts of their desks right up against each other so they could face one another. Their secretary worked in an office outside in the same basic office setup Butol had. Except Butol had his own office.

In their office, out of ear shot of anyone else, Bert and Ray entertained themselves jabbering about jokes they had played on

Butol. They called him B.O., but not to his face. After a while it was mostly Bert who kept the banter going against Butol.

"Hey Ray wasn't that a great idea, that joke we played on B.O.?"

Bert was standing, then walking around the room. He held a pencil that he rolled around in his left hand as he sauntered around the room looking at Ray once in a while. Bert had a habit of tilting his head one way then the other as if there was a weight shifting around inside his head making his skull flop one way then the other.

"Ray. I'm talking to you," Bert said.

Ray looked up from his desk at Bert who had stopped in one place. Bert's head was leaning heavily to the left. Once Bert had gotten Ray's attention he started wandering around the room again. He began to softly chatter almost to himself.

"The guy has got to be embarrassed by now. I can just imagine the look on his face when he saw those shorts. His secretary apologizing while she acted all innocent. Hah! What a scene. That guy is a real jerk nimrod."

Ray was already looking back down at the work he was trying to get done.

Bert noticed Ray not looking at him, so he dropped his pencil onto Ray's desk, then put his hands down on the top of his own desk as he leaned over towards Ray.

"Ray," Bert said a bit ominously as he looked directly into Ray's upturned eyes. Bert then shook his head back and forth a few times as if he was trying to control some kind of heavy loose material that was sloshing back and forth inside his brain cavity. "Don't you think it was a great idea?"

"Yeah I think it was a great idea," Ray responded. "It was great." Then he looked back at his desk.

Bert stood back up to walk over to the window.

"I think it was the best idea we've had so far. I can't wait to hear what the secretaries will be gossiping like," Bert said.

Bert sat down opposite Ray.

Ray looked up to see Bert laughing quietly to himself. Bert's head was moving from side to side, nodding front to back like it was on a spring. Ray smirked, just maybe he thought, Bert's moving head had been the real life inspiration for the bobble-head.

Bert was smiling. He looked quite happy.

Bert spent the morning waiting for the results of the inter-office banter about the shorts. He waited in vain. Not only did he wait in vain until lunch. He waited all day for some results of the prank. No one in the office said anything about the underwear at all.

Ray breathed a number of sighs of relief throughout the day. Bert got more and more angry.

"That son-of-a-bitch asshole," Bert hissed as he broke another pencil in two.

For the rest of the day Ray kept an eye out for Bert. Occasionally Ray put his left elbow on his desk so he could rub his temple with his left thumb while he rubbed his forehead with his fingertips.

"Uh, Bert. How about going out for a beer after work? Okay?" Ray almost pleaded.

"What, huh?" Bert said is if he was answering from another world.

"Beer, b-e-e-r," Ray spelled it out. "Looks kind of frothy like warm horse piss except it's cold. Comes in cans, bottles and kegs."

"Fuck-off," Bert said angrily.

"Hey take it easy Buddy," Ray said. "I'm not the enemy."

Bert shook his head. "Yeah I know. I'm just pissed off."

"So let's wash down a pizza with a few beers. Get a full belly and have a pissing good time," Ray suggested.

"Sure, why not?" Bert said.

At the end of the day they grabbed their stuff as they headed out for food and beer. When they got into the elevator Dick Millstone was already inside. When the two men entered the elevator Dick folded his arms across his chest then placed his right foot onto the back wall of the elevator while propping himself up with his left leg.

Bert and Ray both glanced at him then at each other. Dick looked from one to the other of them when they glanced at him. Nobody else got on the elevator and none of them said a word as the elevator made its non-stop descent to the lobby.

Dick waited for Bert and Ray to exit the elevator. When the door opened at the lobby level neither of them looked Dick's way. Dick kept the elevator door open so he could watch them cross the lobby to the exit door. He watched the two men spin their way through the revolving door to exit out onto the street. Then he pressed the close door button so the elevator could continue its descent to the basement parking garage.

As they walked down the sidewalk Bert said to Ray.

"I want to see him squirm. Even if it's only one time. I want to see what he's really like Ray," Bert tried to explain.

"What do you mean?" Ray asked.

"I hate that he ignores us. It's like he really doesn't care if we exist or not."

"Yeah I know what you mean. It's like he really doesn't care what we do. Like nothing fazes him. I'm getting pretty tired of trying to have fun with a guy who doesn't cooperate. I mean he must have gotten rid of those shorts without anyone else even seeing them. It didn't work like we thought it would."

"That's exactly what I mean Ray. I want to do something he can't ignore. Something he's got to react to. He's got to have some kind of feelings about our jokes. I'm tired of being ignored."

"Yeah, but that inspires you Bert. My tired of it is boredom. The hell with it I say. If he doesn't care then neither do I."

"That sounds pretty chicken shit to me Ray."

"Chicken shit, horse shit, dog shit, it's all the same to me. That's all we get from old B.O. The whole prank thing is getting to be a bullshit waste of time. I'm tired of joking around with him. It's boring," Ray said.

"Boring?" Bert said surprised. "I'm not going to let that arrogant asshole get away with it anymore man. He's got to pay."

"Pay?" Ray asked. "Pay for what? What the hell are you talking about? What is it really with you wanting to get at Butol? I thought it was fun for a while. He doesn't, so let it go I say."

"Let it go?" Bert said loud and angry. "I thought we were friends."

"Friends? What does being friends have to do with playing tricks on our boss?"

"Nothing man. I'll do it myself."

Ray stopped walking.

Bert stopped walking a few seconds later. Then he turned to look back at Ray.

"What have you got in mind? You're getting all cooked up over nothing," Ray said.

Bert furiously retorted. "Nothing? You call his constant ignoring of us nothing?"

"It sounds like we're the ones trying to bug him. We're the ones trying to get his attention. What did he ever do to us?"

"Forget it Ray. It's nothing to you."

"Yeah. You're right. It is nothing. Nothing but attempts to get his attention, which only makes us look stupid for acting like kids. It would be different if he wanted to participate, but he doesn't. So let's call it quits."

"I'm going back to the office."

"Oh come on Bert. I'll buy."

"Buy your own beer. I forgot to do something."

Ray shrugged then continued on to his favorite pizza place. He turned back to see Bert heading back the way from which they had come.

Bert muttered to himself. "I always end up having to do stuff by myself. Shit. I'll let him go get drunk by himself. Ray's another one of those guys like my old man who can't follow through with anything."

Bert began thinking about his dad. The man who would come home late at night drunk with liquor and anger. Bert would sneak out of his room when he heard his parents. He would peek around a corner from the hall to see his father forcing Bert's mother to stand on a coffee table in the darkened living room. The man would point a flashlight at his wife, then order her to take off articles of clothing, then put them back on. He would make her stand still in varying degrees of undress while he turned the light off and on. He would shine it first in one place then turn it off. He would move the light then turn it back on to surprise himself to see what new area he lit up.

When his wife cried he got angry telling her he would go kill Bert if she didn't do what he said.

She always pleaded. "I'll do whatever you want. Don't hurt Bert."

Bert was too afraid to make a sound. He watched terrified and fascinated at the same time.

As the years went by Bert's father drank more and more and kept mistreating his wife more, and more often. Sometimes Bert stayed in his room. More often than not he would watch.

No one in Bert's family ever said anything in the daylight about what happened in their home at night at least once a week for years.

Bert's mother took great care to make sure Bert was well behaved, well-dressed, an all-around good boy. She tried to make up to Bert for his father. The man she married never used to hurt her. In the beginning of their relationship she knew he loved her. She felt deep down he really loved her, that his drinking and making her perform was a phase. But, he kept on coming home drunk to make her perform for him. She couldn't understand how this man that she felt deep in her heart loved her, could continue to hurt her more than she thought it was humanly possible to endure. This man was her husband, the father of their only son, Bert, who was her joy, her comfort, her reason to live.

Bert's father had been a very successful businessman. He was popular, outgoing, well liked. He always took his wife and son to company parties where he could show them off to all the people he knew. But, he never forgave his wife for getting pregnant on him. He did treat her well at first. Then his feelings of confinement gnawed at him until all he wanted to do with her was to punish her for ruining his life. He told her over and over he had never wanted any kids. When he was sober he was an outstanding citizen. He only tortured his wife when he thought it was necessary to punish her for having had his son.

Except for public events Bert's father rarely spent time with him. After Bert was seven or eight he only spoke to Bert to command him to do something or another.

Bert wanted to punish his father like his father had punished his mother. Bert owed his life to his mistreated mother. He knew he would have been happy at home alone with her. He never was. Bert and his mother slowly adjusted to the unacknowledged secret war being waged in their house. They both knew they were being abused. She knew Bert was suffering constantly. Bert knew she was in pain all the time. Neither of them talked to each other about how they felt and would have never dared to tell anyone else. They each knew if they ever talked about what was going on they would have to do something about it. It was fear that kept them from acting on what they knew; because, if they were to do something about their situation they would have to do something drastic.

When he was old enough Bert's dad sent him to college. Bert worried about his mom being home alone with his dad. One day in his senior year at college Bert got a phone call that his mother had died. It was the funeral home trying to give notice of her memorial service.

Bert found out from the funeral director that she had had a heart attack. Her husband had called 911 because he hadn't known what else to do. Bert's dad told them he didn't want to move her. She lay dead on the living room floor next to the coffee table. Her hands were up near her bare breasts, she was clutching a royal blue silk blouse. Bert's dad told everyone he could who showed up at his house to retrieve her body including the police, "She must have been changing a light bulb in the ceiling fixture over the table." It was obvious she had taken a hard fall. She was bruised up, but nothing was broken. The coroner's report stated that she was probably dead by the time she hit the floor. The funeral home director told Bert about the services. She was to be cremated. The man told Bert she didn't suffer. Bert hung up on him.

Bert did not go to the funeral. About two weeks after he had received the phone call from the funeral home, he went back to his room in the dormitory to find a cardboard box and an envelope that had been sent to him by his father. In the envelope was a check along with a typewritten unsigned note stating this was all there was left of Bert's things. Bert never went back home. He never wanted to see his father again. After Bert finished college he travelled around Europe for a year. He came back to work in the United States, eventually got a job at Broom and Williams.

Bert was full of rage during his walk back to the office. He wanted Butol and he wanted him bad. He didn't know what he was going to do to him, but he was going to do something. When he thought of what to do to Butol he couldn't help but think of his mother.

Many times Bert thought of his mother as a gentle loving person. He would remember the tender times they had. Then thoughts of Butol quickly flashed into his head. Attractive, quiet, with a perfect family. The guy was unflappable living his perfect life. Then Bert thought of his mother. He wished she had defended herself. He wanted her to stop letting him be the reason she let his dad torture her all those years. Bert knew he himself was the reason she let herself be humiliated and tortured. He didn't want Butol to be tortured either. He had to get Butol to stand up for himself. The very thing he wished his own mother had done.

Those years when he hid next to the corner of a cupboard to watch what his parents were doing. He would sit transfixed, appalled, horrified, mesmerized, thrilled, and terrified at what he saw on display. But, all those times he never ran into the room screaming for his dad to stop. Bert knew he let things happen. He had never defended his mother. He felt guilt, rage, shame, anger, and pain. He knew he had been complicit in her suffering. He had also been paralyzed by confusion and fear as he felt powerless to defend her. As he got older he realized he had also been too much of a coward to take a chance. She had saved his life, kept him from harm, while he hid. Bert and his mom were so afraid of what her husband might have done they passively participated in their own persecution. As a kid Bert had been trapped and powerless. As Bert got to be a teenager his dad didn't abuse his wife when Bert was home. Now that Bert was older, an adult, he knew he couldn't let things like that happen to anyone anymore. Bert didn't want people to be treated like he and his mom had been treated. He would think of something to make Butol defend himself, something he couldn't ignore.

Bert felt sorry for himself and his mother yet he resented her for setting him against his father. He knew his parents did not get along. They used him to mediate their own disease. Bert wanted to hate his mother for keeping him from loving his father. He wanted to hate his father for torturing his mother. He wanted to hate them both for setting up a situation in which he could not love either one of them. Bert felt like he loved his mother. He wanted to love his father. It was their relationship that made his head spin. For years he would fume and fuss himself into a frenzy.

"I'll fix that Butol. I know how to make him talk. I'll get a gun with a silencer."

Bert went into a gun shop on the way back to the office. He bought a nine millimeter semi- automatic hand gun with a silencer. It was easy to pass the background check. They told him he could pick up his new gun in a few days. Now that he had kind of a plan, he was in no hurry for the weapon. He decided to catch Butol on a day when everyone else was gone.

The office routine went on as before. Except Ray and Bert drifted apart. Ray would ask Bert how he was. Bert would give intentionally vague noncommittal answers. Ray stopped asking. The two of them stopped talking altogether about Butol. Ray was amazed and relieved.

Bert waited until the right day. It had been a couple of weeks since he picked up his handgun, ammo, and silencer from the gun shop. He bided his time until he knew Butol was going to be alone working late. He offered to help Butol. Butol was glad to have Bert help him.

Butol had become convinced his strategy of ignoring Ray's and Bert's pranks had worked. Bert and Ray had not played any tricks on him in weeks. It seemed as if he had let the two of them boil in their own oil long enough. It was like the heat had gone out of the fire that made them want to cook up ways to bother him. Butol had been upset by their pranks, but the only person who ever knew that was Dick Millstone. What Butol didn't realize was that Bert needed Butol to react to him. Bert had to have it.

Butol scheduled an evening to work late with Bert. Everyone else was gone home for the day. Butol was in his office waiting for Bert when Bert knocked on his door.

He got up from his desk to open the door for Bert.

"Come on in Bert," Butol said as he smiled at Bert.

Without saying anything Bert walked in with a briefcase, sat down in front of Butol's desk in one of the guest chairs. He kept the briefcase on his lap below the top of Butol's desk.

Butol walked around to sit in his own desk chair facing Bert.

"Thanks for helping me Bert. It'll be great to get caught up on a few things as well as to bounce around a few things we can do to make things better here," Butol said.

"Yeah," Bert said. "I know a few things that can make things better around here."

"I'm sure you have a lot of good ideas," Butol responded.

While Butol was speaking Bert opened his briefcase with his left hand. The top of the briefcase faced Butol so Butol could not see what Bert was about to take out of the briefcase. Bert pulled the handgun with the silencer out to rest it against his right thigh. Bert closed the lid of the briefcase then set the empty case on the floor next to the left side of his chair.

Before Butol finished speaking Bert raised up the nine millimeter semi-automatic handgun with its attached silencer from next to his thigh so he could point it directly at Butol, whose innocent smiling face was straight across from him, not more than four feet away. The lamp shining on the desk was the only light on in the room. The single light turned the window behind Butol into a black mirror. Bert could see Butol directly in front of him as well as the rest of the room reflected in the window.

Butol, no longer smiling, sat bolt upright in his chair. He took a deep breath. Then he began to sweat.

Bert grinned. "How does it feel to be the helpless one Butol? How does it feel to be powerless?"

Butol barely able to speak, replied softly, "What Bert?"

"You heard me," Bert snapped back.

Butol didn't say anything.

Bert began to feel good. He liked the feeling of power that began to wash over him. Memories of his mother and father came to his mind. Images of himself hiding behind a cupboard door, sneaking looks at what his parents were doing.

With his left hand he stroked the barrel of the silencer he was pointing directly at Butol. The gun was heavy for him so he rested the butt on the desk.

Bert said, "Talk to me Butol."

Butol's pulse was quickening, he kept sweating. Bert had caught him completely off guard. Butol started to quiver.

"Talk to me Butol," Bert demanded.

"Yeah, sure Bert. I'll talk to you about anything you want to talk about," Butol said. "Sure I'll talk to you."

Then it happened. Bert regressed, he became himself when he was two, then when he was four, then ten years of age. His mind clicked him over into a role he had been forced to play out as a kid.

Suddenly he said to Butol. "Why did you do it dad?"

Butol was relieved and horrified at the same time. He realized that Bert had lost contact with the present reality. He realized Bert was talking not to him, but to his own father. Then Butol realized he knew virtually nothing about Bert's family. He also wanted to stay alive.

"I'm not sure what you mean Bert," he tried to explain.

"Don't play innocent with me. You know exactly what you did."

Knowing he had to think fast Butol said, "I'm sorry I did it Bert."

"Sorry? Great," Bert said sarcastically. "Like that makes any difference."

He raised the gun up off the desk holding it with both hands.

Butol sat stock still.

"Don't move, don't blink. Just sit there while I think," Bert ordered.

Butol slowly nodded his head.

"I know what to do," Bert told Butol.

Bert grabbed the bright lamp from Butol's desk with his left hand while maintaining his grip on the gun with his right. Then Bert pushed his chair back away from Butol's desk with his legs while he kept the gun pointing at Butol.

Bert gave his head a shake then seemed to come back to the present.

"Get up on the desk Butol. Push all that junk off onto the floor and stand up on your desk," Bert told him.

Butol straightened his right arm out across the top of his desk. Then with one sweeping motion wiped everything toward his right off the desk onto the floor.

"Up you go," Bert told him as he pointed both the gun and the light at Butol.

Butol hesitated.

"Do as I say. Stand up on that desk!" Bert commanded.

"Take off your shoes and socks," Bert told him.

Butol obeyed.

"Okay now your shirt and tie."

Butol complied.

"Now dance for me."

Butol shuffled his feet and moved his arms a little.

"Now be still."

Butol stopped moving.

Bert quickly clicked the light off, then back on.

Butol winced, blinked his eyes.

Butol thought, I'm in a fantasy dream where nothing matters, except this. This is all real to Bert.

"Take off your pants and shorts."

Butol obeyed.

Bert turned the light off and on while Butol dropped his pants onto the desk. Then he slowly pushed them onto the floor with the toes of his right foot.

Bert kept turning the light on and off.

The noise of the light clicking on and off could not drown out the sound of Butol breathing fast.

Bert kept the light on as if he was examining Butol. Then he would turn it off.

Butol was alternately bathed in the bright light of the high intensity desk lamp or enveloped in moonlight. At times the room was completely dark except for the pale moonlight softly cloaking the naked man standing still on his own desk.

For long moments neither man spoke. Then Bert kept the light on for what seemed a long time.

All of a sudden Bert fired a shot into the front of Butol's desk.

The sound of the wood cracking made more noise than the silenced gun.

Butol jumped into the air, slipped as he came down then groaned as he fell hard onto the dark maple desktop. He twisted his right ankle and hit hard on his right hip when he fell. When he landed on his right side he was facing directly at Bert.

Bert watched in silence.

Butol cried out, "Why are you doing this Bert?"

"Shut up," he cried. "I'm teaching you a lesson!"

Bert started looking around the room as if he thought someone else was in the room.

"I thought I saw somebody," Bert said. "Did you see someone behind me?"

"No. I can't see anything except that damn light!" Butol exclaimed.

"Did someone come in?" Bert asked.

Butol, knowing he was helpless, remained quiet as he waited on Bert.

"You know why," Bert said. "You hired me. You know all about me."

Butol closed his eyes. "Why are you so angry at me?"

"You act exactly like my parents. That's why," Bert hissed at Butol.

Butol squinted in Bert's direction trying to see him behind the bright light.

Then Bert went on as if he were ten years old talking to his best friend. "My dad used to hurt my mom. My mom let him do it to protect me and I watched them the whole time I was growing up. I didn't do anything to stop them."

Butol closed his eyes. He let go of the right ankle he had been rubbing so he could lie down flat on his back.

Bert kept talking. "I wasn't even home when my mom died. I never protected her. I don't know what happened to my dad. He sent me money when she died."

Butol kept still.

Bert let out a few deep sighs. He was like a locomotive at the end of a long day running down its tracks. An overtired engine coming in slowly to the station while hissing off its last bits of steam.

Butol didn't move or speak.

Bert kept the light and the gun trained on Butol.

"All I wanted you to do was stand up for yourself," Bert said quietly.

Butol asked. "You wanted me to stand up for myself? Like your mom?"

"What?" Bert asked.

"Yeah, you and my mom," Bert exclaimed.

Bert quickly stood up as he threw the lamp and the gun into the front of the desk where he shot the bullet. The room went dark when the bulb in the lamp shattered as the lamp slammed into the desk.

Bert slumped back down into the chair.

The room was quiet again. With the inside lights off the moonlight coming in through the window softly bathed the room in a wash of pale blue.

Butol could hear Bert softly crying.

The two men stayed where they were for about a minute until Butol gingerly crawled off the end of the desk away from Bert. His ankle winced when he stepped onto the floor. In the moonlight he hobbled over to the door to his office. He locked the door between his and Linda's office. Then he turned on a ceiling light controlled by a rheostat, about a third of the way up. In the dim light Butol looked at Bert. Bert was holding his head in his hands as he sat quietly in the guest chair facing Butol's desk. Butol could see the broken lamp and the gun lying on the floor in front of his desk. He walked over, careful to avoid the glass from the light bulb, to pick up the gun. Butol carefully took out the clip and emptied the chamber of the nine millimeter gun before putting it in the lockable top drawer of his desk. Then he grabbed his clothes off the floor so he could put on his pants and shirt. Bert didn't move from the chair.

Butol sat down in his own desk chair.

"Bert," Butol began. "I'm not sorry I didn't fight you back. I know I ignored your practical jokes. I didn't want to get myself mixed up with that kind of behavior. I thought you didn't like me. I'm so sorry I didn't listen to what you were trying to say to me."

Bert sat still.

Butol went on. "I thought you had something against me. Now I know it wasn't me at all. I promise you the next time somebody leaves a dirty pair of underwear on my office door I'll try to find out why."

Without looking up, while he still held his head in hands, Bert said, "Okay, thanks."

For the first time in a long time Bert's head was still.

The End

CADILLAC CAB

The only thing I ever really wanted to do in life was drive a Cadillac cab. I wanted to drive people around in one of the finest cars in the world. Certainly the finest car to come out of Detroit. I wanted to drive a Cadillac cab; because, I believe with all my heart everyone needs to be pampered for a time, at least once in a while. Jeffrey they call me at home, or Dad, or Honey, but at the shop where we keep the cabs of the Green-to-Go cab company where I work everybody calls me Jeff and-a-half. We've got three full-time drivers day time and two part-timers at night, one of whom is our on-call guy. Which means he, the he being me, or she Cindy, only drives if there is overflow. But, lots of time old Jeff and-a-half will take up that slack to stay for a longer shift. Which is why they call me Jeff and-a-half. I spend a lot of time driving people around, day and night.

Holidays and the like we're all busy. Our little company operates in the central Washington city of Yakima. If you're ever in town and need a ride from the airport or anywhere else for that matter all you have to do is call Green-to-Go. We'll be waiting for your call at our shop on the corner of Front and Walnut streets in the heart of downtown. We can get anywhere in the greater Yakima area in a matter of minutes. I can make it from as far as Terrace Heights, the farthest eastern part of town, to West Valley in less than ten minutes. That might be only right after the bars close at two in the morning, but I think you get the idea. I like to think I'm the best driver in the company, but that wouldn't be fair to my fellow drivers.

So there's me, Cindy, Willy, Donald, who we call The Drake because of Donald Duck and The Duke, John Wayne, which is hard to explain to someone who hasn't worked together with us as long as we have. Which is since 1966, about ten years now. We're still driving our two Kelly green Chevy four door Impalas and our one two-tone, blue-on-top, white-on-the-bottom Chevy Bel-Air station wagon. Which is by far the best car we have to get you at the airport. It has the most room and the best seats. We all share doing the dispatch job too. We don't all get to drive all the time. But, it always works out okay. Everybody has to do it, so it's fair.

We also have a spare car. Which I don't like to drive and like less talking about. It's an okay car. The thing is it used to belong to Daryl the-ding-bat's mom. We all call Daryl, who owns Green-to-Go, Daryl the-ding-bat. Not to his face of course, but he knows we've called him that because he's overheard us talking in the shop. Daryl the-ding-bat not only owns the place, he does all the mechanic work on the cars. Which is a good thing and a bad thing. He started the business when he got some money after his dad died. It so happened when he hired us on in the beginning none of us figured we would be driving his cabs for as long as we have.

To the surprise of most people in town who know anything about Yakima, the cab company flourished. At the time we were the only cab company in town. People got used to having cab rides. Daryl, who we called Daryl the-ding-bat for starting a company everybody thought would fold in a couple of months, started making some real money. Even though his company took off the name stuck. Which is why we still call him Daryl the-ding-bat. The thing is he's a lot smarter than most people think. When somebody like him has a good idea nobody believes in them until it works out. Then when somebody like him succeeds the people who thought he was goofy get mad and jealous wishing they had thought of it. If it fails people say it was a stupid idea. But, if someone like him succeeds then everybody gets on the bandwagon and says how good of an idea it was. It's like the phone, even electricity. Now we take those things for granted. Cabs too.

So anyway Daryl the-ding-bat's mom's old car is a 1953 Ford sedan. It's two-tone, like the Bel-Air wagon, but different colors. The Ford has a dark green top and a yellow body. It's in perfect shape for a car that makes you feel like you're driving a boat on land. The thing handles like you're trying to drive a cork in a bathtub, which you can't. The original flathead engine is in perfect shape. The car only has about twenty thousand miles on it. Daryl the-ding-bat keeps it in the garage in case one of our other cars can't be driven. When Daryl the-ding-bat's mom died he told us he had this car he didn't feel comfortable getting rid of. So one day about a month or so after she died he pulled it into the garage and parked it in one of the same stalls where we keep the other cars. Even if we don't use it for work he takes it out once in a while for a spin.

What we don't have is any Cadillac cabs. Not a single one. And the way things are going I doubt if Daryl the-ding-bat will ever get us one. I think the biggest reason we don't have any Cadillac cabs is Daryl the-ding-bat, who is a mechanic's mechanic, doesn't want to work on a car as fancy as a Cadillac. He says it's got too many moving parts. All that electrical stuff is only "more junk to go bad", I've heard him say.

Then there's Willy. All the time we have a lot of fun with Willy. When it's slow and we're just hanging around the shop we make jokes. I bet we've made a million jokes with Willy's name. We're always saying things like: will he do this, or will he do that, all kinds of things. Almost every day I ask The Drake. "Hey Drake, what do you think? Will he make it here on time or will he be late again?"

The Drake always laughs. Which I always enjoy because The Drake has kind of long hair, not hippie long hair, but over the collar hair combed back, kind of greasy, real smooth, with a little flip at the base of his neck, that looks like a duck's tail feathers. Anyway when he laughs he kind of wags his head back and forth like a dog which makes his hair flop back and forth with every wag. So while his hair gets to-moving the snorting he always does when he laughs gets going too. He's the snortingest, hair swingingest, sucker I know. I love to get him going in the morning 'cause that will get him to swinging his arms so he usually ends up spilling his coffee which tends to hit his pants in the front making it look like he peed himself. By the time Willy shows up we've been having a good time waiting. Sometimes I think Willy comes in a few minutes late just to see if The Drake has spilled coffee on the front of his pants yet. It's all pretty funny because we actually have uniforms to wear and The Drake will have to change if he gets himself all messed up.

Daryl the-ding-bat insists we wear the Kelly green pants and shirt uniform when we drive. He won't let us drive without it. He has our names sewed on the right upper part of the chest. Each of us has a white oval about four inches long and three inches high with two inch tall letters of our name embroidered in bright red to contrast with the green shirt. On the back of the shirt is the company logo "Green-to-Go", embroidered inside another white oval shaped patch. The company letters are about five inches tall embroidered in the same Kelly green color as the company shirt. We've had to wear these uniforms since the beginning. Daryl the-ding-bat started us wearing them from day one. He buys them, pays to have them cleaned, repaired, and replaced whenever they need it. When we first started out, Willy, The Drake and I all thought having the uniforms seemed kind of weird which also made us think of Daryl as a ding-bat. But, we quickly learned that looking professional, clean, and tidy made us a lot more money. I wish I had a nickel for every compliment I heard about our clean cabs and uniforms. Maybe I got the nickels in tips already, but I know looking sharp always helped us out.

We all have keys to the garage too. We've had to have them. Daryl the-ding-bat had to give us keys so he wouldn't have to open up the place when he didn't want to. Which in the last few years has been more and more frequent. He pretty much comes in only when we have a broken car. Which isn't very often.

Then there's Cindy. Cindy is our bookkeeper as well as our night time fill-in, on-call driver person. She started at "Green-to Go", about a month after the rest of us. Daryl the-ding-bat introduced us to her one day as the bookkeeper to whom we had to give all our paperwork. He told us he didn't want to do the bookkeeping anymore because he didn't have time. She was going to be handing out our bi-weekly checks too.

Cindy, we all think, is about ten years older than the rest of us which makes her about forty-five or so. Nobody I guess, except her high school friends knows for sure. I'm never going to ask her. She's pretty tough. She's smart and independent as anything. Is she a worker? If she isn't keeping track of Daryl the-ding-bat's books at the garage she's driving for him nights. Plus if she isn't taking care of "Green-to-Go" stuff she's putting in time as a part-time teacher at a school where her daughter's kids go. She works there helping the regular teacher keep things straight. I know I don't sleep a lot, but I don't think Cindy ever sleeps. That's pretty much all any of us knows about Cindy.

Excepting one thing, we never call her anything but Cindy. Even when she isn't around we call her Cindy. Because, there was one time when we were milling around the garage trading off cars and such, that The Drake was as usual, joking around about Willy when he happened to mention Cindy. He knew Cindy is all business and not a big talker, but for fun this one time he calls her Windy-Cindy. He was being sarcastic, about her not being so talkative, you know ironic about her talking. The poor guy was trying to be funny. For about two weeks, I swear she didn't say more than three words at a time to any of us. For that whole time when she did talk it was all small words, except for The Drake. All she said to him was "jack-ass", for the entire two weeks.

We all thought it was funny for the first day or two, her calling him a "jack-ass". But, after a week of us all figuring out that the only words she said to him were "jack-ass". Well it got to be not so funny. It wasn't just the fact that she only said "jack-ass", to him it was how she said it. Which was like this.

We could all be standing around in the garage between shifts. She would be less than three feet away from The Drake. She'd look him straight in the face then use her voice in a little more than a whisper to say "jack-ass". Well of course The Drake thought it was funny at first too, but then he started getting scared of Cindy. None of us knew quite what to do about it. What we didn't do was joke around with Cindy. We all called her Cindy. We gave her our paperwork. We were real polite and nice. When she gave us our regular two week paychecks she handed me and Willy our check by saying "pay". She silently handed The Drake his check, turned her back on him then while walking away she said, "jack-ass."

We all looked at each other kind of weird like. The Drake gave a big sigh. Willy and I kept quiet until Cindy left the garage in the Bel-Air wagon for her shift. She didn't even look our way as she slowly drove past the three of us on her out of the garage. That was a Friday evening. When Monday rolled around we were all finishing up again when Cindy comes in to take over for Willy who had been in one of the Impalas. The Drake had been driving the Bel-Air all day. I'd been doing dispatch in our trade around way. We all had CB radios in our cars so it was pretty easy to keep in touch. Well Cindy comes sauntering into the garage with a big smile on her face. She tells us all how beautiful the day is. We're acting all nervous like when she starts talking to The Drake like she used to. As if the two weeks previous had been some episode of "The Twilight Zone", or something. It was like those two weeks of her saying nothing to him but "jack-ass", hadn't existed.

It was scarier than when she wasn't talking to The Drake. She taught us all a huge lesson. I'm not sure I got it completely, but after those two weeks we knew to never make fun of Cindy. That was just the way it was. We all got it. Ever since that time we call her Cindy, nothing else.

So that pretty much rounds out the situation at Green-to-Go. Except for the problem of not having any access whatsoever to any Cadillac cabs. I've been looking into this situation for quite a while. Like I said before I want to give customers a quality ride. The best possible ride I can. I don't think I can do that in a ten-year-old cab that seems like it has a million miles on it. There isn't anything wrong with our cabs. All our cabs are in great shape. The only thing is that not a one of them is a Cadillac.

Don't get me wrong. I don't want to sound greedy. We don't have to have an all Cadillac fleet. We only need one Cadillac to pamper people who need it. Although it does seem unfair that only one driver could offer the service of riding in a cushy Caddy. It would be better if we had an all Cadillac cab company. We could call it "Cadillac Cab Service". Or "Cadillac Cab Company", even "Cadillac Cab", that would work. Wouldn't that be nice?

A person could arrive in town from having visited their relatives in Tokyo. Think of it. They've been travelling a real long time, changing planes and such. They're tired, cranky, hungry, thirsty, and anxious to get home. Or maybe somebody had to go to a funeral of someone they loved. Maybe they're coming back from Vegas where they got married and divorced in the same weekend. As a cabbie, even in the town where I work I've seen plenty of people return from trips where they wished they'd stayed home. People get really stressed in life. Sometimes you think you know what people are really like, but they surprise you when all they do is call someone "jack-ass", for two weeks.

So anyway, in my mind, I picture a beautiful Cadillac that pulls up in front of a person's house or the airport to whisk them off their feet to transport them wherever they want to go. And I mean regular people, who pay regular rates, not really rich people who ride around in limousines. We would have a cooler built in to the back seat or something. We would have cold drinks, snacks, some fruit or something for people to enjoy. I could let the people into the back of the car, watch them sink into the luxurious back seat where they would have blankets, a couple of pillows and all the room they need to relax. Maybe they'd curl up like a baby for the last leg of their long journey. Wouldn't that be nice?

I've been driving cabs for more than ten years. I've never ridden in the back seat. If I was riding in a cab, I'd like some place to feel comfortable, even if it's only for a little while. I'd like to be pampered, secure in a place where no one is going to bother me. I could have an apple, a drink of water, an ice cold beer, or whatever. Someone else would be responsible for everything that happens, at least for a little while. I'd like that. I think everybody would.

The End

CHULI AND YO-YO

This story is about a spider named Yo-Yo and a ten-year-old girl named Chuli. Chuli and her baby brother live with their wheelchair-bound grandmother in a trailer house that sits amongst a grouping of what most people call a trailer park. The places are called parks not because they consist of open fields of green lawn with children's attractions, like swings, climbing toys or have a swimming pool with water, but because at one time the homes were pulled there and parked, usually never to move again. The park where Chuli lives shares a property line on the north and west sides of a Seven-Eleven which sits on the busy corner of two four lane arterials, Sixteenth Avenue and Fruitvale Avenue, in Yakima, Washington. East across the street from the Seven-Eleven store and gas station which faces the intersection of Fruitvale and Sixteenth Avenues, is White Pass Garage. Across Fruitvale south of the garage is a Cooper tire store, while west across Sixteenth from the tire store is a used car lot. This is the immediate neighborhood which Chuli calls home.

On a warm late spring day after school Chuli's grandmother asked Chuli to set a sprinkler in the tiny four-by-six foot patch of weedy grass she called her backyard. Chuli went outside like her grandmother asked her. She began to unwind the garden hose off the hanger reel attached to the back of the trailer house. To her great surprise she saw a black jumping spider dangling from a string of web attached to the hose. The more hose Chuli pulled from the reel the more the spider bounced up and down on its string of web like a yo-yo. So she named the spider Yo-Yo.

"Hey Yo-Yo! You better get off this hose or you might get pulled somewhere you don't want to go."

As soon as she said that, Yo-Yo, using her spider string, slowly descended about a foot onto a three-foot wide, four-foot-long sidewalk right next to the trailer, which Chuli's grandmother called "the patio". Yo-Yo landed on some of her back legs then settled onto all eight of her legs. Then she waved her two front legs in the air as if she were saying thanks to Chuli. Chuli could see tiny blue spots on top of Yo-Yo's head as well as a white mark on her back that all together looked like Yo-Yo's body was making a face the size of her whole body.

"Hey, Yo-Yo you're so cute. Do you want to get to know me? I'm putting the sprinkler on the lawn for my grandmother. If you are still here when I get back maybe you can be my pet spider."

Chuli took her time setting the sprinkler in place so the lawn and flowers in her grandmother's flower box garden would get watered at the same time. As she walked back to the house she could see Yo-Yo walking around on the cement sidewalk.

"Okay Yo-Yo, if you're still here when I get back from finding a jar to put you in you can be my pet spider."

As if to say okay, Yo-Yo lifted up her front legs and waved them around.

"You look like my baby brother when you do that. When he wants someone to pick him up he waves his arms and legs too," Chuli explained to Yo-Yo.

Chuli went into the house. She found an empty plastic mayonnaise jar with a screw-on lid. She brought the jar outside to show Yo-Yo. Yo-Yo had walked over to the edge of the sidewalk to stand in the crack between the cement and the bottom edge of the house.

"Do you see this jar Yo-Yo? This will be your home if you still want to be my pet spider. You could breathe and crawl around. You could play and eat all you want. If you still want to be my pet spider you have to remember this jar will be your whole world. Once you go in the jar you will have to stay inside there until I let you out. That way I can see you whenever I want to."

Yo-Yo kept still in the crack next to the house.

"That is what it means to be someone's pet you know. I would be in charge of you. I would take care of you. I would feed you, give you water, and visit you. You think about that okay. If you still want to be my pet you wait right here."

Chuli went looking around on the ground outside of the house for things to put in Yo-Yo's new home. She found some leaves and sticks so put them inside the jar. When she came back she did not find Yo-Yo waiting on the sidewalk for her. She got down on her hands and knees to search for Yo-Yo, but did not find her anywhere on the ground.

Chuli stood up to look. She saw Yo-Yo dangling from the hose reel. Yo-Yo was bouncing up and down like she was when Chuli first found her.

"Yo-Yo it looks to me like you want to be my friend, but not my pet. I think that is a good decision. I am sure we would both be happy if I could come outside and see you being yourself bouncing up and down on your string instead of me watching you stare at me from inside this mayonnaise jar."

Chuli unscrewed the lid from the mayonnaise jar while she walked to the end of the patio. Then she crossed the four-by-four-foot area of gravel where her grandmother kept her lawn tools. Chuli turned the jar upside down to let the sticks and leaves fall onto the ground next to the fence that separated her trailer from the one next door.

When she came back onto the sidewalk to talk to Yo-Yo she found Yo-Yo had climbed up on the hose reel hanger.

"Will you be here tomorrow if I come to visit you?"

As if saying yes, Yo-Yo raised her front legs up and down.

"I'll see you tomorrow then. I'm glad you want to be my friend," Chuli said. "I need to go in the house now to help grandmother with dinner."

Chuli waved at Yo-Yo. Then she went back in the house to put the mayonnaise jar back where she found it. After that Chuli went into the kitchen to help her grandmother with dinner. Chuli smiled as she looked forward to tomorrow's visit with her new friend.

The End

CURLY

Caroline's face pleaded with him to stop. To let her go. She had tried to get away. Curly could never forget the look she gave him. The look that meant she would never tell anyone what he had done to her. The eyes that told him if he would let her go he would be forgiven. He knew every eyelash, freckle, and line in the face he had not been able to resist or forget.

Curly rolled over against the wall of his cabin. It was a bright sunny summer Sunday morning. He pulled the wool blankets up over his face so he could try to go back to sleep. Caroline's look, the memories he had of her, pushed him from one town to another, from one job after another for thirty years. No matter what he did he hadn't been able to rid himself of that look. He loved that beautiful girl, hadn't wanted her to die. But, he had killed her. He couldn't forget the way her mouth opened when her head, too heavy to be held up by her broken neck, fell loosely toward her left side to rest obliquely near the top of her left shoulder.

The memory of being in the car with her haunted him. It came to him when he was working, when he was walking down some highway, when he was having a good time with other traveling workers like himself. As if out of nowhere a memory of Caroline's face or body would flash across his mind's eye. He would be resting at a bus station or listening to directions some farmer was giving him and a group of co-workers where to meet for the next day's work, when Curly would spot a clock on a wall that told him exactly what time he had killed her. An unexpected clock would remind him of the time she died. For more than thirty years he kept telling himself he hadn't meant to do it, while Caroline's face and time itself seemed to follow him everywhere.

Curly whose name wasn't Curly then, had picked Caroline up on the way home from basketball practice at the high school where he was her social studies teacher. He knew her well. Every day he was stunned by her beauty. He tried to treat her like he did every other student. It wasn't easy. He tried to not encourage himself about how he felt about her. Charles was smitten with the way she looked. Simply by being who she was Caroline had enthralled Mr. Charles Watson. Mr. Watson was a happily married man, but found himself irresistibly attracted to a beautiful, wholesome, and innocent sixteen year old girl.

Mr. Watson had been teaching at the Catholic high school for six years. It was his first teaching job since he attained his Master's Degree in education. He was a good teacher. The students liked him. He got along well with all the other faculty and staff. Except for the coaching duties after school which Charley didn't want to do because of his family, his career was blossoming. The principal told him it was okay that he didn't coach; because, Mr. Watson had young children at home.

Charles, who preferred being called Charley since it seemed friendlier, happened to stay late one afternoon preparing tests that signaled the approach of Christmas break. From his office he could hear the girls' basketball team practicing in the gym. When they finished in the gym his office got quieter, which made it easier for him to work. Within fifteen minutes of the end of the basketball team's practice he finished up. He was ready to give the tests the next day.

Mr. Watson went out to his car to drive home. He pulled out of the lot, then drove a few blocks toward his house when he noticed one of the girls from his school walking on the sidewalk. She was wearing her school uniform, white blouse and dark blue skirt. He thought maybe it would be a nice thing to give a ride to a student who had to be out in the cold walking home in the dark.

He pulled up alongside the girl who he thought might be Caroline. The girl stopped to look at a car coming to a halt next to where she was walking. Charley put down the electric window on the passenger side. Caroline looked in the car from where she stood on the sidewalk. She smiled when she recognized Mr. Watson.

"Hi! Mr. Watson."

"Hi Caroline. Are you all right? Walking home by yourself on this late afternoon? You must be cold."

"Yeah, I forgot my coat today. I'll be sure and wear it tomorrow. We get pretty hot and sweaty playing basketball. I forget how cold it is after coming out of the locker room."

"I bet."

"I'm okay."

"That's good. I saw your school uniform and thought I should stop to give you a ride if you needed it."

"Well, I am pretty cold. You wouldn't mind?"

Charley smiled, then said. "That's why I stopped."

"It would be great if I could get home a little earlier. My dad should be getting off work pretty soon. My mom has me cook on Thursdays because she has to work until six."

"Well then get in I'll get you there in plenty of time."

Caroline got in the front passenger side of the warm car. She put on her seat belt. They started off.

"You'll have to give me directions Caroline. I have no idea where your house is."

"Yeah sure, well I live on Twenty-Seventh Avenue about a block off of Lincoln Avenue."

"I think I know where that is," Charlie said.

"Great," Caroline said.

Charlie glanced back and forth between Caroline and the road. He wanted to stop the car so he could look at her.

"That's pretty far from here. I might have to make a stop on the way if you don't mind."

"Okay."

Charley found himself breathing a little faster. Not a lot, but he knew he was excited to be alone in his car with this beautiful girl.

"I'm going to stop at the mini-mart on sixteenth and Lincoln to pick up something for dinner at my house."

Caroline nodded, then said, "Okay."

Charley pulled in on the side of the mini-mart. The store lights lit up the parking lot in front of the store. The side of the store where he parked was a little darker, a little quieter. Even so, inside the car Charley and Caroline could see each other clearly.

"I'll be right back," he said.

Charlie went in the store, then waited around for the other two customers to leave. By the time he got back to his car he could see no else was around. His was the only car near the store and he knew the only person left in the store was the clerk.

Charley had purchased a quart of half-and-half. "We use it for coffee at home," he said as he got in the car on the driver's side.

He sat behind the wheel on the driver's side for a few seconds. Then he reached over the top of the seat to put the container of half-and-half on the back seat of the car. After he put the container on the back seat with his right arm, he repositioned himself near the middle of the front seat.

Charley looked squarely at Caroline. Unable to resist her beautiful face he softly took hold of her head with both hands. He felt her luxurious hair between his fingers. Caroline froze. He kissed her on the lips.

Caroline's heart was pounding, she broke out in a sweat. She didn't know what to do.

Charley kept kissing her on the mouth.

All of a sudden Caroline tried desperately to get away. Charley held her head tighter. She tried to pull herself from his grip. The seat belt kept her from moving her lower body. She tried violently to twist her head away from Mr. Watson's grip. There was a loud cracking sound in her neck. Her head slumped in his hands. He let go. Her head fell obliquely toward her left shoulder nearly touching the headrest on the back of the seat. Caroline went limp.

Charley had been holding tightly to her head as she struggled. When he let go he pulled his hands away from her. The palms of his hands still faced her as if he was giving her some kind of macabre blessing.

Charley looked out the car's windows. He didn't see anyone. He let loose Caroline's seat belt so he could position her in the front seat. He pulled her toward the steering wheel so she looked like she could have been sleeping. He got himself out of the car, then looked around the area. The car was beeping. He quickly grabbed the keys out of the ignition then dropped them on the floor. He took all the cash he had out of his wallet before tossing the empty wallet onto the floor near the keys. Before shutting the door he pressed the electric lock. He looked at Caroline's dead body lying on the front seat of his locked car. Her face was turned toward the floor. He kept looking around, but didn't see anyone. Then Charley walked away. He kept on walking.

Charlie walked to the outskirts of the town where he was a respected family man. He made it to a freeway on-ramp where he hitchhiked a ride with a salesman heading northeast. He told the man the first of many stories filled with lies. It was in that pack of lies he told the salesman that Charley Watson became Curly Gray. In less than an hour's conversation Charley Watson had changed his complete history. After a few hours driving time, the salesman stopped for the night at one of his routine motel stops where he dropped off his hitchhiker. He had no idea who Charley really was. Charley it seems had died when Caroline did. In the front seat of a small sedan, under the dim light outside some quiet mini-mart, that could have been in a town almost anywhere in the United States. After delivering the man he knew only as Curly nearly two hundred miles from his home the salesman checked into a nice motel and bid Curly adieu. Charley Watson was gone.

Curly kept going. He checked his pockets. He had a little cash, forty-two dollars total, one twenty, one ten, two fives, and two ones. Since he left his wallet in the car he thought maybe people would think he had been the victim of some random robbery or kidnapping. After all, never before had he done anything remotely like he had just done. At the time he thought now I know why some guys end up riding the rails to nowhere. Spending their lives becoming more and more unknown to anyone.

For thirty years Charley lived as Curly Gray. He travelled from place to place every way imaginable. He hid in plain sight in tiny towns, on ranches or farms, as far as he could get from people he thought might find him. He did a good job of living as someone else. That was the easy part. Carrying Caroline with him for thirty years was the weight that wore him out.

The cabin he found himself waking up in at the Smith Ranch on Sunday, his day off, was the last one he hoped he would have to endure. Curly had travelled as far as he wanted to go. He wanted to set Caroline down. To let her go. The only thing was she kept appearing in his dreams. He wasn't sure if it was dreaming of Caroline that woke him up in the little cabin he was living in at the Smith's ranch where he had been working as a farm hand for a little over a year, the longest job he had ever had, or some noise in the distance he usually didn't hear on a Sunday morning. Either way he had gotten used to the scratchy wool blankets he wasn't ready to come out from under on his day off. Someone told him they were army surplus. He didn't care, they kept him warm.

Charley Watson had transformed himself into Curly Gray. Eventually the name he picked fit him. He was now in his middle fifties. His face was rough, leathery, bearded in light gray. His hands were muscled, calloused, and hard. Curly had kept moving all those years to stay hidden from a past he thought would never leave him. Caroline appearing in his head had become his steady companion. His memory of her was awash in dreams he had never fulfilled. Since he left his home he had no idea what became of his wife and kids. As far as he knew they did think he had been robbed or kidnapped. No one ever seemed to be looking for him. If it hadn't been for his memories of Caroline he thought he could have always been Curly Gray. The day he walked away from Caroline lying in his car was the day he might as well have been living in a different universe.

The truth is he wasn't living in a different universe. He was living in a place where he could keep warm, get plenty to eat and stay out of harm's way. Curly had succeeded in becoming as close to being a no-one as a person could be. He had no identification, social security card, or bank account of any kind. He had depended on employers to pay him cash. Which he had not always been able to collect.

Here at the Smith's they liked him. Pearson Smith the son of the owner, who lived on and ran the ranch, was a rebel kind of a guy who had all kinds of people working for him from time to time. He didn't like to do manual work himself so he was glad to have a-nobody-kind-of-guy like Curly around to do what he didn't want to do. Even though it was Sunday when Curly wasn't supposed to work Curly could hear Pearson's yellow Can-Am quad ATV coming his way.

"Doesn't he have anything better to do than bother me on Sunday?" Curly said. Then he got himself out of bed and was mostly dressed in his work clothes by the time Pearson arrived outside the front door of his cabin.

Pearson skidded to a stop in the soft dirt in front of Curly's cabin. He left the motor of his four-wheeler running while he yelled at Curly.

"Hey Curly?" Pearson hollered.

When Curly swung open the cabin door its hinges gave out their usual squeal.

Curly squinted at Pearson because the sun was directly behind the young man who called his name. Curly cocked his head to his left side while he held his right hand up above his forehead to shield his eyes from the piercing sunlight.

Pearson laughed as Curly strained to look at him. "Too early for you on your day off old man?" Pearson said.

Curly nodded. "I'm not a kid like you Pearson."

"Kid? What do you mean kid? I'll be twenty seven in two months. My dad is thinking about making me a full partner pretty soon. I won't only be ranch manager anymore. I know it's your day off. I thought you might like to do something fun." Pearson said. Then Pearson spit a big gob of Copenhagen juice out onto the ground. As usual a small thin string of spittle stuck on his chin that he wiped off with the top of his left hand, which he then wiped off onto the left pant-leg of his 901 Jeans.

Pearson was wearing his beige sweat-stained Stetson cowboy hat, white alligator skin Tony Lama cowboy boots that stuck out from under his Levi's 901 button up jeans. His school-bus-yellow Hard Rock Hotel Las Vegas t-shirt had the short sleeves cut off so everyone could see the full color six inch tall tattoo of a rampant cougar Pearson had on his right deltoid.

Curly smiled at Pearson. "What have you got in mind Pearson?"

"How about going fishing with me? There'll be somebody else there. It won't be just you and me."

"Who?"

"A neighbor," Pearson said.

"When?"

"When? Well right now."

"I haven't eaten yet."

"Don't worry. I'll feed you. We'll have coffee, all the fixings, you know."

"Let me grab my hat," Curly said.

Curly went into the cabin to retrieve his favorite hat. He put on the dark blue ball cap with the white New York Yankee logo on the front he had gotten a while back, a year or two, maybe more, at some free meal place after he had been found naked and beaten in a gutter. He had forgotten most of what had happened to him that landed him in that gutter. Someone had beaten him up, taken all he had, including his clothes and shoes, then left him lying naked on the ground. He remembered being picked up by a man dressed all in black with a little white thing on his neck who had helped him. The man helped Curly, whose vision and knowledge of where he was at the time was very vague, stand up. Curly, who could only see out of one eye at the time due to his beating, realized the man was a Catholic priest. The priest wrapped Curly with a blanket then took the Yankee cap he had on his own head to place it onto Curly's head. The priest smiled at him, hugged him, and took him inside some building where he was given a chance to clean up, get some new clothes and eat. There were quite a few street people in the building where the priest brought him. If it hadn't been for there being so many people in that place Curly probably would have stayed longer. The priest was always good to him. Curly wished he had been able to stay, but felt it was too dangerous for him. He thanked the priest for all his help. Then when Curly felt healed up enough he left. He was only at the priest's shelter for a few days.

"Love your hat Curly," Pearson said.

"Yeah, me too," Curly said. "How many times have I told you I'm not giving it to you?"

Pearson grinned.

Curly made his way up onto the back seat of Pearson's four wheeler. Pearson leaned back onto Curly. "Ready to rock and roll?" Pearson said not expecting an answer. Then he gunned the machine back up toward the main ranch house. The knobby tires churned up a pretty good sized cloud of dust behind the ATV as they drove up through a few rows of Bartlett pear trees. When they arrived in Pearson's driveway Curly could see a girl sitting on the tailgate of Pearson's lifted F-250 four-by-four pickup. She was holding a tall brown bottle of Budweiser in her right hand while she had her left elbow on top of a cooler. She was beautiful.

Pearson stopped beside the truck on the driver's side. He got off first. By the time he got to the back of the truck where Rachel was sitting she had an open beer ready for him. He took it from her. Then she recoiled from him when he tried to kiss her on the mouth. Pearson laughed at her. Curly walked over to stand about ten feet behind the truck while Pearson got in the cab.

"Don't be shy Curly," Rachel said. "I'm not. We're neighbors you know. I live on the Hampton ranch next door."

"I've heard of you," Curly said. "Nice to meet you."

Rachel was wearing a red and black plaid western shirt. Like Pearson's t-shirt Rachel's shirt had the sleeves cut off. She wasn't wearing a bra. She left the top three buttons of her shirt undone. Her voluptuous breasts hung freely filling from behind the two snap pockets of that untucked western shirt. Her mid-thigh jean shorts were unbelted. At the end of her long tanned legs she was wearing white Nike cross trainers with short socks.

"Ready for a beer Curly?" she said.

"No thanks. I don't want any beer. How old are you?"

"I'm seventeen. You think I'm too young to have beer. You know Pearson and me are neighbors. It's only friendly to have a beer with your neighbor."

"Uh-huh. I don't drink. There are lots of ways to be neighborly."

Rachel set her beer down so she could lean forward off the tailgate to step down onto the dry dusty ground. Her long brown hair fell loosely over her shoulders. As she leaned down Curly could see the smooth skin inside her shirt. She stood up straight to stretch her nearly six foot tall frame toward the sky. She reached up alternating both arms like she was picking fruit out of the air with her slender fingers. Curly watched her move. Rachel was between him and the back of the truck, so Curly could also see Pearson grinning in the rearview mirror.

Curly watched as Pearson came around to the back of the truck with his beer.

"We've got everything we need in the back of the truck. Hop in so we can go. We're going to miss fish breakfast if we don't get out of here."

Pearson got back in the cab of the truck. Rachel sat in the middle of the bench seat. Curly had the shotgun seat next to the window. Curly sat as close to the door as he could. Rachel put her feet down onto the floorboard next to Curly's. The smooth skin of her legs pushed up next to Curly's work pants.

Pearson drove out past the house toward the lake. It was a nine mile trip on gravel, then dirt, then mostly rocky, rough terrain near the lake. Even with their seat belts on Pearson, Rachel, and Curly bounced up and down as they also bumped back and forth into one another. Rachel bumped into Curly while he tried to keep from bumping back into her. Every once in a while she put her right hand on his left thigh and her left hand on the dash to balance herself. In order to keep as far as he could toward the right side of the cab Curly crossed his left arm over his chest so he could hold onto the top of the door with his left hand while he grabbed hold of the mirror bracket on the outside of the door with his right hand.

The day was getting warmer. The three of them were starting to sweat. Curly kept smelling Rachel's perfume mixed with her sweat. When she turned toward him he could smell a slight odor of beer-breath. Rachel was stunningly beautiful to Curly. He smiled back at her when she turned toward him to give him big grins as they bounced around on the seat. Curly couldn't help but look at her chest bouncing along with the rest of her. Her hair flew back and forth from the hot wind coming in through the open window. Occasionally she tried to hold it back with her left hand while she held onto Curly's left leg with her right hand for support. When Curly looked over at Pearson he could see Pearson smiling along with the two of them. Curly knew Pearson didn't need to drive like he was in order to go fishing.

Curly tried looking out the window a lot. Along with some yellow Balsam there was a lot of sage brush still in bloom. He spotted an occasional rabbit. Once in the distance he thought he had seen a coyote. It wasn't easy to keep his eyes off Rachel.

Pearson seemed to enjoy making Curly uncomfortable by doing all he could to throw Curly and Rachel together. He drove the truck faster than necessary and went over bumps he could have avoided. The things in the back of the truck got tossed around as much as the people inside. Like a kind of mischievous little boy Pearson was clearly enjoying himself.

"We'll be there in a couple more minutes," he said loudly over the grinding, winding sounds of the truck. He was grinning and nodding his head.

They drove over a rise in the road when all of a sudden as they headed downhill the lake appeared about a hundred yards right in front of them.

"See, there it is," Pearson said.

The lake took up about two acres in the bottom of a small valley rimmed with sage brush and various grasses. There were a few cottonwood trees opposite them trying to stake a claim on the bank of the lake. While off to their right about halfway around the lake was a rocky area that stood in contrast to the surrounding terrain. Some of the big rocks jutting out of the ground were over ten feet tall. The rocks formed their own secret hideaway, a kind of ellipse with sections between the rocks where a person could easily pass. If you stood in the center of the rocks you couldn't be seen from outside them. People had to pass between the standing rocks to enter the open area inside their wall. It was a very secluded spot about thirty feet across.

Pearson drove up within about twenty feet of the secluded rocky area to park the truck. He turned off the big V-8, set the parking brake.

All of a sudden it was quiet. The three of them sat still inside the truck for a few seconds while the dust settled. They were enjoying sitting on the soft seat they had been bouncing around on for the last forty minutes. Rachel let out a sigh. The hot truck made various ticking sounds as it cooled down. They could hear a meadow lark call out.

Pearson got out first. He went around to the back of the truck to open the tail gate. Curly opened his door, stepped onto the dry dusty ground then turned to face inside the truck so he could prop open the door for Rachel. Her hair fell forward as she pushed herself from the middle of the seat toward Curly. She stretched out both arms to him. He looked up into her inviting face. Curly put his hands up under her arms to help her out. When her feet touched the ground Rachel was standing with her face about six inches away from him.

"Thanks, Curly," she said. "You're a lot stronger than you look."

"Sure," Curly said as he backed away from her.

Pearson was taking fishing rods, a tackle box, and a cooler from the back of the truck. He got the cooler out so he could set it in the shade.

Rachel and Curly walked to the back of the truck.

"Here," Pearson said handing Rachel another long neck Bud.

She took it in silence.

"Here, Curly," Pearson said as he handed Curly the tackle box and fishing rods.

Then Pearson pulled an army green duffel bag from the back of the truck. He carried it over to the rocky area where he disappeared between the rocks. Curly and Rachel were putting together their fishing gear when Pearson came back from the rocks.

"A guy I know said to use power bait for trout, and plugs for bass. So there's supposed to be both kinds of fish in the lake," Pearson said.

"Sounds good," Curly said.

Rachel rolled her eyes, "Whatever works."

Pearson laughed.

"Ready for another beer?" Pearson asked.

Rachel shook her head no while she held up the beer he had just given her. Then she said. "I'm still feeling that first one and I have this second here."

"That's good isn't it? I mean why drink beer if you don't feel it?" Pearson said.

Curly looked from Pearson to Rachel and back. Then he started working on his fishing line again, getting the hook right, putting the power bait on the hook so it wouldn't fall off.

Pearson got another beer out of the cooler for himself. "Nice and cold," he said.

"What's wrong Pearson? Not going to fish?" Curly asked.

"What do you mean?" Pearson said.

"You're not getting ready to fish," Curly said.

"I don't know. It's such a nice day I might wait a while," he said.

"Do you think it's too late in the morning to catch fish?" Curly asked.

"Hard to say."

While the two men spoke back and forth Rachel was tying a plug onto the end of her line.

"Going to catch some bass, huh?" Curly asked.

"That power bait stuff stinks. I don't want to touch it," Rachel said.

"Bass are good eating if you can catch them," Pearson said.

"Mm-mm," Curly mumbled.

After getting the plug on her line Rachel took an occasional sip from her second beer of the day.

"So where are the hot spots in this lake?" Curly asked.

"I don't know Curly," Pearson said. "I think I'm going to wait a while. Drink a couple more beers. Watch you guys, see if you catch anything then try my luck."

"Okay," Curly said. "What about you Rachel?"

"Me?"

"Yeah you. Do you know how to fish this lake?" Curly asked.

"Maybe," Rachel said.

"Okay you two. You've both lived here a lot longer than me. I think you're not telling me what I need to know so I can catch a fish or two here," Curly said.

Pearson said, "You know Curly they say there's fishing and there's catching. Then there's the beer drinking and laying around. I think I'm going to wait on the fishing and catching for a while." Then he walked off toward the rocks.

When Rachel figured Pearson was out of ear shot she gave Curly a big smile, then said. "My dad used to fish this lake when he was a kid. He told me to try a green plug like this one I put on my line. He said to cast it out, let it settle a little, then reel in a little at a time. At the same time you're supposed to wiggle your rod up and down a little to set action into the plug."

Curly laughed. Then he told her, "You sound like you've been doing this for quite a while young lady."

She smiled back. "More than I want Pearson to know. He likes to think he's smarter than everybody at everything. He's so into himself it isn't funny."

Curly nodded, then said, "Is that right?"

Curly opened the cooler to find nothing but beer and ice inside.

"You work for him. Isn't that the way he treats you?" Rachel asked.

"I don't want to say too much, he's right over there behind those rocks. He can probably hear us. I'll tell you this. There's no food in that cooler. All he brought was beer and ice."

"I don't think he can hear us. Who cares anyway? Let's see if we can catch some fish out of this old lake."

The two of them started walking down the slight slope to the lake.

"Yeah, good idea," Curly said.

"I don't know about this mid-morning fishing thing," Curly said. "I always thought it was better to fish real early in the morning or way late in the evening. You know, sunrise or sunset. I'm going with the power bait. Way less work."

"Well, there's fishing and there's catching Curly," Rachel said as she winked at him.

"So did you finish that second beer already?" Curly said.

"No, I only drank a little to be sociable. I left it on the tailgate. That one I had while I was waiting for you guys to show up at the truck was the earliest time I've ever had a beer. I think that goofy Pearson wants to get me drunk," Rachel said.

"I think you're right," Curly said.

"I know he's already had at least three. He had one when I drank that one back at the house. Then he had another one when he brought you up to the truck, and he's already finished off the one he started here. He's probably loopy by now."

"Yeah," Curly agreed.

"So I'm going to pull this plug along over here in front of that little bit of brush near the edge of the lake. Why don't you toss your power bait out over there toward the middle of the lake?" Rachel said.

"Sounds good," Curly said.

The two of them were fishing separately in different ways about fifty feet from each other.

Curly sat down on the bank waiting for a strike from whatever might enjoy eating on his power bait. Rachel walked a little to and fro as she cast her plug in the lake, reeled it in, cast it out again, to reel it in again.

The day was warming up as the sun got higher and higher in the sky. A few fleecy clouds floated high overhead. When no one was talking the only sounds came from nature. There were a few meadowlarks calling, a grasshopper would occasionally flit up into the air making its short lived imitation of a "Huey", helicopter. The lake gave a hint of moisture to the dry air. Curly could feel a slight warm breeze flowing past him. It wasn't long until he went from a sitting position to watch his fishing rod, to lying down on the warm dirt with his eyes closed. It didn't take long for Curly to fall fast asleep.

It wasn't a fish biting his line that woke Curly. Rachel was hollering for help.

"Stop it Pearson," she yelled. "Leave me alone. Curly are you out there? Help me! Help me!"

Groggily Curly sat up from a deep sleep. He was confused. He hadn't been leaning next to the wall of his cabin covered with his old blankets. He had dirt in his eyes. He couldn't focus. His face had been down on the ground. Rachel's screaming seemed far away. He looked around for her. She was nowhere in sight.

"The rocks," he said.

Curly got up. He ran as fast as he could over to the rocks. He found an opening and made his way between two of the large upright stones. In the middle of the ring of stones Curly could see the cooler along with some towels, blankets and beer bottles on the ground. There in the center of the ring of stones, standing next to all the things on the ground, were Pearson and Rachel. Curly was facing Pearson's back left shoulder. He could clearly see what Pearson was trying to do.

Pearson had a tight grip on Rachel. He had his right hand wrapped around her upper left arm while he gripped her upper right arm with his left hand. Rachel's hands were down at her sides. Pearson had overpowered Rachel. He was in control of her. Her shirt was down around her waist. Her shorts were halfway down her thighs.

"Shut up Rachel, that rotten old bastard wouldn't dare help you. He wants you too. I saw him eyeballing you," Pearson said.

While Pearson was hollering at Rachel neither of the two noticed that Curly had appeared from between the rocks.

Quickly Curly bent down. He picked up a jagged rock about the size of a ripe cantaloupe. Curly ran up behind Pearson faster than he had ever run before. While Curly ran he lifted that sharp, jagged, cantaloupe sized rock that fit perfectly in his right hand, high over his head. He was still running when without a hint of hesitation Curly brought his high right hand with that rock in his tight grip directly down onto the back of that young man's head. There was a loud crack from Pearson's skull. Pearson's eyes crossed, his knees buckled. His grip on Rachel was gone. Pearson fell to the ground. Curly tossed away the bloody rock.

Rachel stared at Curly. She hurriedly tried to pull up her shorts. Then tried to wrap herself in her torn shirt.

Curly saw her nearly naked body as he pulled a large beach towel from the ground. He couldn't help noticing how beautiful she was as he handed it to her. Pearson's body lay between them on the ground. Blood was oozing from the back of Pearson's head into the dirt. As Rachel wrapped herself in the towel Curly gently touched the top of her towel-wrapped right shoulder to guide her away from the dead man.

As she walked away Curly let go of her shoulder. Rachel started sobbing.

Curly threw a big towel over the top of Pearson's body to cover his torso and head. There was no question the young man was dead. Rachel was right. She had no idea how strong Curly had become.

"Come on Rachel," Curly said. "You need to get out of here. Come on out to the truck."

Curly guided her out from between the rocks. He walked with her to the truck.

Rachel was shaking.

"What are we going to do Curly?"

"We?" Curly said. "We are going to do this."

"You are going to listen to me. You are going to do what I say. You're pretty scratched up. Pearson tried to rape you. You're going to drive this pickup back to your house. You're going to tell your mom and dad what Pearson did to you. Do you understand?"

"Is Pearson dead?"

"Yes, I killed him," Curly said. "You need to listen to me. Do exactly what I tell you. Do you understand?"

Rachel nodded, "Yeah, yeah, okay," she said.

"Are you sure?" Curly asked.

"What should I do?"

"You drive this truck back to your house. Tell your mom and dad exactly what happened. They'll know what to do. You tell them what I did. You don't tell them it was me, Curly. You tell them Charley Watson killed Pearson."

"What? Who's Charley Watson?" Rachel asked.

"Yeah. I know, listen, you tell them this guy Charley Watson did it. He's some guy I heard of whose wanted for murder in another state. If you tell your parents that, they can tell the sheriff. Okay?"

"Charlie Watson?" Rachel asked again.

"Yes, he's a murderer on the run. If you tell them about him we'll both be okay," Curly said.

"Pearson's really dead?" Rachel said.

"He's dead," Curly said.

"So you want me to drive home. Tell my mom and dad Charley Watson killed Pearson to keep him from raping me?"

"Yes, exactly that. You need to go now so I can clean this up," Curly told her. "Pearson left the keys in the ashtray like he always does. I saw him put them there." Curly said as he handed her the pickup keys. "See here they are. Now you get in this truck and you drive away from this mess. Go to your family. They'll see you're safe. Go home now. Don't wait around here."

"What about you?"

"Rachel, now, please, go home. Please!" Curly said.

Curly helped her up into the tall four by four pickup.

"Go, don't worry about me," he told her.

"Okay," she said. "I'll see you later then."

"Sure. Now go," Curly said.

She started the truck to head for home. Curly watched the truck disappear over the rise.

He let out a few big sighs as he looked around the area. The tackle box and his fishing gear were down by the lake. Rachel's fishing gear was nowhere in sight. Curly left everything where it was.

He began walking the opposite direction from the Smith Ranch. He walked and walked until around dusk, when he came upon what looked to be a sparsely used two-lane highway. Curly hitched a ride with a cowboy who was heading from his hometown to a Rodeo in Las Vegas. The passenger seat of the truck was filled with fancy tack. The only place for Curly to ride was in the back of the truck with an old saddle and some scratchy wool horse blankets. Curly rested his head on the saddle seat while he covered up with the old horse blankets.

While traveling in the back of the pickup Curly kept thinking about what he had done to Pearson. Finally he got tired enough to fall asleep after eating one of those ham and cheese sandwiches, from which he had to carefully peel the green and white labelled plastic wrap, and drinking a quart of milk the cowboy bought for him when they stopped for gas during the night. Riding in the back of the truck was noisy, but soothing. The regular sounds of the wind and the constant vibrations of the truck massaged Curly into a deep sleep.

As they passed slowly through another small town along the way that made them slow down to twenty-five miles an hour. Curly woke up. He sat propping himself up with an elbow on the saddle. It was shortly after sunrise. The street lights along the business part of town were all off. As they drove along Curly looked at an old ten foot tall cast-iron clock painted a bright royal blue that stood proudly on the side of what must have been the Main street of the town. The clock read a little after six o'clock in the morning.

Curly didn't feel nearly as tired as he usually did. He woke up refreshed. Like it was a new day. He remembered during his long ride in the back of that cowboy's pickup, a dream he'd had about Caroline in which she was wearing a light blue prom dress while riding a horse uphill through a field of ripe winter wheat. Curly could see bright sunlight illuminating the trail of broken wheat stalks where the horse had stepped. It looked like Caroline was loping her way up and over the hill. Then she stopped. Caroline turned in the saddle to see the man she knew to be Charley Watson standing in the middle of the trail behind her. She smiled, then waved at him. He began to cry. The girl kept smiling while she turned back around into the saddle to continue on her way. Caroline left a glowing mist of sunlit wheat dust in the air as she disappeared over the top of the hill. The man in the dream waved to her until she was gone. When she left his crying stopped.

The man who had changed his name to Curly stretched out his legs under the wool horse blankets as he lay back down in the bed of the pickup. He put his head on the saddle seat like he did before while he lay on his back. As he looked up at the sky he watched the sun change the color of the clouds from grey to purple, lavender, orange until eventually the clouds became their daytime white where all the colors are hidden. The cowboy's pickup gradually sped up as they left the little town. The truck was making its regular noises as it went faster and faster. At highway speed the soothing vibration began. Curly pulled the brim of his Yankee's cap down over his eyes. He held the foot end of the wool blankets with his feet while he gathered the top end up around his shoulders with his hands. He was no longer in a nice quiet cabin. He was wrapped in wool blankets with his hat down over his eyes in the back of a pickup. He was warm, as comfortable as he could be. There was no one to wake him up until his next stop.

The End

HENRY AND SILVER

For a few years my job in Aspen was to make as much money as I could to support my skiing habit. I grew up in Hales Corners, Wisconsin, a suburb of Milwaukee, Wisconsin, which is about ninety miles north and west from Chicago. The ski hill in my hometown is a former landfill with a two person chair lift stuck in its side. I love my hometown, my friends, Wisconsin, the Packers, even the Bears, just kidding. I love everything about where I'm from, I consider myself a real cheesehead. If Wisconsin, Illinois, even Iowa, had mountains I probably would have stayed home. The thing is I wanted to ski down mountains. I needed to go to the Rockies.

I looked at the maps, did a little research and decided to make Aspen my first choice. It didn't matter to me that I didn't know anyone there. Anyone who has ever been to Aspen knows why young people from the Midwest flock there. It's very simple, Aspen has everything. As far as I'm concerned there are no mountains between the Rockies and the Appalachians. So when I got out of school in the spring of 2006 I drove my little old Ford Ranger work truck to Aspen. It only took me about a week. I wasn't in any hurry.

I camped here and there along the way, picked up a few stragglers hitchhiking to various places.

I finally made it to Aspen in the second week of June. I celebrated my birthday before I left with some friends most of whom thought I was crazy for not going back to college in the fall with them. They jealously referred to me as crazy Randy, their token ski-bum friend. I told them they were all chicken for not taking a chance on themselves. They wished me luck.

When I got to town I drove around to rubber neck at everything. I parked as close as I could to the gondola which was a great place for me to ogle Ajax, the mountain on which I hoped to be spending a lot of time. Everybody I ran into seemed pretty friendly. It sort of reminded me of college. There were so many young people wandering around.

I had a little money which I knew wouldn't last long. I needed a place to stay and a job. It was easy to find work. I landed a job painting to start. When I found out how easy it was to find manual labor I struck out on my own doing odd jobs. It only took me a couple of months until I snagged a couple house-sitting jobs for people who wanted someone to watch their place while they were gone. I got some good referrals and was doing great. Those of us who did jobs like that had a pretty good little network to let each other know what was up. I heard of a guy who was looking for someone to do a bunch of different odd jobs for him. I called him to set up an appointment. He said he'd give me a try. Within a couple of weeks of doing all kinds of things for him I kind of became his go-to guy.

Henry Hancock hired me to do some little things at first. The first time I went out to his place I knew I had to be careful. Never before in my life had I been to a place as cool as his. He lives in this New England looking mansion place a little west of town surrounded by literally acres of lawn and pastures. The house is huge, about ten thousand square feet not counting the five bay garage. He has a big white steel shop building with a blue roof, a horse barn, corrals, and a couple garden sheds out near the perimeter of the lawn where the tennis court is.

When I pulled into the parking area I put my pickup with its nose facing the shop. I didn't think it would have looked good to pull up right in front of the house. I got out of my truck to look around by going around to the other side of my truck. Then this guy came out of the little swinging shop door. Without looking directly at me he sauntered up to my pickup on the passenger side where I was standing.

I looked him over as he approached me. He stopped about ten feet in front of me. He looked to be about fiftyish or so. His hair was wavy, dark with silver, what I always thought of as distinguished. He looked like a model. He was tall, almost lanky, tanned to perfection, clean shaven, he smelled good, like some kind of wood. He was wearing a set of what looked like new white "Osh-Kosh" overalls. Which I had only ever seen displayed on mannequins in department store windows or on college students when I was at home in Wisconsin. I mean who wears white overalls? I know they make them, but nobody who buys them actually wears them to work in, do they? They get so dirty so fast. I've known girls who wore them to school and like that. This guy looked so clean I wondered what he had been doing in the shop. His hands looked like he had never done a lick of manual labor in his life. He seemed to be in good shape. When he did directly look at me it was over the top of a pair of reader type glasses.

"Are you the guy who's supposed to be here?" he asked.

"I hope so," I said.

"So your name is Randall Williams?" he asked.

"That's me," I said as I put my hand out to give him a shake.

He did not shake my hand. Instead he reached up to remove his glasses so he could put them in a triangular shaped case which he then put in the left upper chest pocket of his clean white coveralls.

"I don't do that," Henry said.

"Okay, you're the boss," I said.

"Yes, well," he said. "I have some yard work for you to do."

"Great, I'll get right on it," I said.

"So when can you start?" he asked.

"Now," I said.

"Good, that's good. I had a man working here for a while. He left a couple of days ago without finishing his work. I was disappointed about that."

"Tell me what to do. I'll get started right away."

"Good."

"I can do a variety of things," I said.

"We'll see," he said. "Over there," he said as he pointed to a shed at the edge of a lawn about a hundred feet away, "you will find some tools with which to clean up the area around the pool that didn't get finished."

"Okay, will do," I said.

So started my career working for Henry Hancock. I got my gloves out of the truck then set off for the shed. I spent a couple of hours raking and hauling away brush and grass from a spot near the pool shed which had been cut, then left in what looked to be a half-finished way. There was stuff strewn around like it had been blown in a strong wind. I don't remember there being a wind storm in the last couple of days. I cleaned it up. I also gave myself a little tour of the place which was a blast. I found the tools for cleaning up around the pool, looked at what I could easily see of the house while I was working around the pool area. What I didn't do was check out everywhere. I did what Henry wanted me to do then I went back to where I had parked. While I was doing those chores I couldn't tell you where Henry went until I went back to my truck to get a drink and a snack.

Once again he appeared from the shed like some kind of ghost. He had a pair of binoculars in his left hand.

"So do you think you could do more work for me this afternoon?" he asked.

"I can be here all day if you want me to."

Henry nodded his head like he was thinking about something else. "Okay, good. I might want you to do something else after you finish lunch."

"I can be finished now," I said.

Henry gave me a kind of smirk then said. "I have something to do for a couple of hours. I'll pay you for your time if you wait here until I give you your next assignment."

"I'll be here," I said.

When he came back he had me move some things around parts of his yard, do a little grass clipping and bush trimming, things like that. At the end of the day I was at my truck when he reappeared again.

"So do you want me to pay you for today or at the end of the week?"

"You want me to work the rest of the week?"

"If you want to. I've been keeping an eye on you. What else can you do?"

"I can work on small engines, do some maintenance on bigger vehicles. I can paint, do carpentry, landscaping like I did."

"How about bicycles? Can you fix flats?"

"On bicycles? Sure, no problem."

"I can give you some work if you want it then," Henry said.

"Sounds great to me. What time should I be here?"

"Tomorrow come at nine, in the morning. We'll see how it goes."

"Okay, nine it is," I said. Then I remembered to not try a handshake.

Pretty soon he was having me come over to his place to work on all kinds of stuff. He had me repair his flat bicycle tires. When the regular stable guy was off he had me feeding his horses. It was great to have steady work like that doing all kinds of easy jobs. Plus I was making a lot more than I would have made being a prep cook, waiter, or something else in one of the cool restaurants in town. He started me maintaining some of his equipment, even some of his toys. He had a Viper that he raced, some snowmobiles, a couple of four wheelers, two Harleys, one for him and one for his wife, Lucinda. He also had various lawn mowers, trimmers, even chain saws. He had quite a bit of stuff that looked like it had been used at one time then abandoned. He didn't have me do any work on the Viper. He had specialists for that. Anyway all the other things he had for me to do kept me pretty busy working only for him. It seemed that the more he had me around the more he liked me. Which was pretty cool.

It wasn't long before I was spending most of my weekdays at his place. Once in a while he wanted me to do something on weekend days too, which was fine with me. I always showed up when I was supposed to. I did exactly what he wanted done. Which I found usually makes bosses happy. It didn't take long for me to earn Henry's trust. Something I always felt good about. I thought I had it pretty good working for him.

After I worked for him a couple of months he let me see more of him. Not that we became buddies, because with Henry it was always Henry, he didn't fraternize with the help. On a rare occasion I did see him trying to work on some of his stuff. I was walking past the open garage one day when I saw him flinging stuff around. I heard a couple of hard knocks where some tool he threw hit the inside wall of the garage then clanged down onto the cement floor. I didn't want to embarrass him so I turned around like I was heading out to the yard.

This situation working for Henry went on regularly for months. I was there most days so much I saw other workers coming around to do stuff he wanted done. He always had more work than I could have ever done on my own so it was good he hired professionals to do work that was beyond me. He had a team of people who came to work on his Viper to get it ready to race and to be his support team at racing events.

I started working for Henry in the summer and kept working for him through the winter. By the time early spring came around he was talking about going away for a couple of weeks. He asked me if I would house-sit his mansion, feed and water his white Cockatoo named Silver, and generally keep an eye on things while he took his wife and daughter on a trip. They were supposed to be gone two weeks. Henry told me since it was pre-tax season this trip was to be part vacation, part business. He laughed as he told me he had to visit with accountants and lawyers to figure out how much he wouldn't be paying in taxes again this year.

It seemed to me it was the only two weeks I had ever seen him make much of an attempt to prove to himself or anybody who cared, that he actually performed some kind of task or another to justify what he did for the rest of the year; which, was to play tennis, bike, ride his horses and race his Viper in the summer, or ski, snowmobile and party in the winter. Once in a while he threw in a few things here and there like school activities for Trina his daughter, such as going to plays she was in. He told me she was a very good actor, but primarily his wife Lucinda took care of kid stuff.

Anyway, Henry trusted me, which made me feel good. He wanted me to be at his place for two weeks to make it look like somebody was living there, keeping an eye on things. It seemed like a pretty good deal to be there when Henry wasn't. The best thing about it was he wasn't going to be hiding in some secret place staring at me with his binoculars while I worked. One of the main daily chores was to be sure Silver was okay.

I was elated when he asked me. It was going to be great to have the whole place all to myself. With all the time I spent around Henry's place I noticed quite a few things about Henry that he probably didn't want other people to know. I found out some of the real reasons why he had to have so many people do all these jobs for him.

Over the course of a few months I discovered Henry was pretty bad at most things. He was a mediocre tennis player. He played people much older than him so he stood a better chance of winning every time. He often had fake injuries that kept him off his bike. His horses were too tall for him. Once in a panic when we were alone in the stable he told me he was terrified of falling off a horse at anything more than a walking pace. Which doomed his personal polo career to owning a non-competitive team. As far as racing the Viper, well, he actually did that. He told me when he would be racing so I would go to see what he did. Each race I got to see him in he would try a few laps. He would get passed by all the other racers until he would come into the pits to become once again a DNF for what he usually said was a heat related thing in the cockpit or some mechanical issue. So much for Henry's summers. I never knew him to finish a race, in any sport. He was a mediocre skier even though he had the best outfits.

My first winter in town I worked for him when the World Cup downhill ski racers were in Aspen for their annual tour event. Henry wore a spider web pattern downhill racer uniform pulled up above his right knee to show people he had sustained a recent injury. I happened to be near the base of the gondola with a couple of my skiing buddies. We went to watch some of the qualifying and practice runs. I was wandering around at the bottom of the mountain near the finish line. I looked over near the medical safety area. I happened to see Henry limping about in his spider web downhill racer outfit. He wasn't wearing any racer numbers; however, he was showing off a nasty abrasion I knew he sustained two days before when he fell getting out of his Escalade in the parking lot of an expensive restaurant.

I had been doing some minor window repair at his place when he told me he caught his left arm in the seat belt as he was getting out of his car. He got turned around by the belt, slipped on some ice, then fell to the ground onto his right knee. He sustained a four inch long by two inch wide abrasion which he had treated at the emergency room. When he made some excuse to me about not being able to get around very well with his injury, as if he now had a real reason instead of some kind of excuse that was keeping him from any type of manual labor he would have never done anyway, he peeled back the big white bandage they put on his knee at the emergency room to show me his parking lot scratch.

I was surprised when I saw Henry hanging around the base of the mountain in his spider web pattern ski racing outfit with the right pant leg rolled up. He had taken the bandage off giving the impression he had been recently injured. I had seen people, ski racing fans, walking around near the medical unit looking at the bloody knee he must have picked at to make it look worse than it was; because, when I saw it for the first time, it was a big scratch. It looked to me like Henry was trying to let people know he was an injured racer left unable to compete due to his misfortune. All I can say is when I worked for him around the time of that year's world cup, being in his presence made for an interesting couple of weeks. It was like that injury had sidelined him from all physical activities. He didn't even ride his snowmobiles that winter.

It was interesting to see how Henry dealt with people he hired. He would watch them work like he did me the first day I worked for him. He'd watch us paint, mow the grass, fix his stuff so he could try to use it. Henry had no patience with fixing things. He would start in then get frustrated. Sometimes, not often he would yell at some worker he didn't like, but he would only say a word or two, something like "stop!", or "that's enough!" When it came to Henry telling a worker to stop, stop meant drop what you are doing, leave my property never to return. I have seen Henry walk up to a person, look right at them and tell them to leave his property immediately.

There were also plenty of times when it looked to me like Henry was going to explode as he walked away from a hired hand or some project. I remember when I was doing some grass trimming near one of the mansion windows I heard what I thought was Henry screaming real loud inside the house. I minded my own business about it especially when only about a minute later I saw him coming up the driveway in his black Escalade. I figured it must have been a TV or something inside the house.

I had been gearing myself up for my mansion sitting job. So when March finally arrived and Henry was supposed to be gone for a few weeks on his business trip, I was stoked. Henry had already let me in his house a few times so I would know where to sleep while I would be staying there. He also showed me his main office where he kept his pet white Cockatoo named Silver.

Silver didn't look too healthy to me. I don't know much about birds, but I figured there was something really wrong with Silver because he had pulled out a bunch of his own feathers. When Henry introduced me to Silver he went to reach into Silver's cage. All of a sudden Silver started shaking like he was scared. I don't know what was going on, but it looked to me like Silver was terrified of Henry. So this was the bird I was supposed to watch while Henry was gone.

By the time Henry left with his wife and daughter for their trip I had been ready to move into their place for a month. Henry gave me keys to the place. I was to have free rein of whatever was in the house. I could eat anything I wanted, sleep anywhere I wanted, watch any TV I wanted, play pool whenever, go hot tubbing, whenever I felt like it. All of which I knew better than to take advantage of.

My bedroom, one of the guest rooms, was pretty far away from Henry's main office. My first night in the house I could hear screaming. I was pretty scared at first so I quickly hopped out of bed to check it out. The screaming sounded like it was coming from Henry's office. It sounded like Henry, who I thought was gone, had come back. I went to Henry's office to find that Silver was now whistling. I thought what a crazy-ass bird. I had forgotten to put his cage cover on so he would sleep. Right away after I draped the cover on his cage he stopped making any noise. I walked around the house to see if I heard anything else making noise. I mean what if Henry had come back? False alarm. I found nothing out of order so I went back to bed.

The next morning I went to water the plants in Henry's office with a garden pitcher. I took the blanket off Silver's cage. I went back to watering until I heard angry swearing. I poured water from the spout of the pitcher onto the floor for a couple of seconds before I turned around to see where the screaming was coming from. Of course it was Silver. It was uncanny. It had sounded to me like Henry had gotten home, and was screaming at me for being in his office. The night before while I was trying to sleep in my guest room I had heard Silver scream a couple times. I didn't really care what the silly bird was doing, besides, by the time I got to the office where he should have been sleeping he was whistling. To hear him during the day, close up, was unnerving.

Here I was in Henry's private office by myself hearing his pet cockatoo scream. There had always been something about Henry I couldn't quite figure out. I know Henry always wanted everything to look good, like everything was classy, and cool. When I was alone in his office for the first time to hear firsthand what I thought was Henry screaming I figured out what it was. I remembered when I had been working outside at Henry's. I had heard what I thought was Henry screaming. When I saw Henry pulling up in the drive I thought the screaming must have been TV, or a stereo. Now I was convinced it must have been Silver.

Silver's screaming was a dead ringer for Henry's screaming. When Henry screamed it sounded like he was screaming at the top of his lungs, so when Silver screamed he sounded like he was screaming at the top of his lungs. If you didn't know it could have been Silver doing all that screaming you could get the impression that Henry was a complete two-faced liar. A suspicion I'd had for nearly as long as I'd known him.

Henry, I mean Silver, but I guess it was really Henry talking through his bird, started to swear and degrade people by name. He called people filthy dirty names saying how stupid and incompetent they were. He made fun of how they looked and talked even saying things like how crummy their clothes were.

That Silver was one smart bird. He had an incredible memory. I was spellbound as I listened to him give away Henry's private thoughts. It didn't take me long to figure out that the longer I waited to feed him in the morning the more he would scream. I figured he was complaining that I wasn't feeding him on time by using Henry's voice to get my attention. The longer I waited the more there was to listen to. I learned a lot from Silver.

I usually fed Silver in the morning about eight o'clock. But, after a couple of days I'd bring in my breakfast, lean back in Henry's comfy wing back burgundy leather office chair to make myself at home and make Silver sing for his food. I found an old cassette tape recorder in one of Henry's office closets along with some tapes on how to get a bird to talk. I decided to record what Silver said. After I figured out how to work the little old cassette machine I set it up with a microphone on Henry's oversize walnut desk. Once I got it going I'd push myself deep into that buttery smooth leather chair while I propped my bare feet on the matching ottoman. With my eggs, sausage links, whole wheat toast and hot sweet blond coffee on my lap tray I'd listen to Silver, but it was really Henry.

I couldn't help it. Since I had free run of the house I had access to all the available food. I'd savor Henry's pure unblended Kona coffee to wash down my organic free range chicken eggs. I ate toast made with the most expensive bread of Henry's I could find. I listened to Silver for hours. It was amazing. Silver's words came out in a wild flood as if a dam of words had broken loose. It was like listening to an out of order audio book. The sentences would be mixed up, chapters were out of order. Occasionally he would be in pause mode. He never paused for long. Except he'd close his eyes once in a while. When he did that he'd go silent for what sometimes stretched into a few hours. I supposed he was sleeping. I let him sleep. Usually I went to sleep too.

It seemed Silver must have heard Henry say some vile things over and over and over; because, Silver repeated himself. He'd start in on something then he'd say it over and over again. It was sentences like "If she ever does that again I'll kill her," said loud and mean that really got my attention. Or things like, "Bob is the laziest S.O.B.", or "Bob's got to be the most useless excuse for a human being I've ever seen." Or plain old, "Bob the bum." "Bob the bum," seemed like one of Silver's favorites because he said it a lot. I'd worked with a couple of Bobs at Henry's. I wasn't sure which Bob he meant, as if it mattered.

It was so obvious that Henry, whether he wanted to or not had even taught Silver to say some of the meanest, nastiest things about people he supposedly loved. People who thought they were close to Henry. People who Henry had convinced somehow that he did love. Like his wife Lucinda. Silver said things about Henry's immediate family no one would want to hear anyone say to any other human being let alone their spouse or child.

Henry's bird was too good a secret for me to keep to myself. Which was too bad for Silver; because, I'm pretty sure Henry was the cause of Silver's premature death.

Quite a while after I finished the house sitting job, a couple of months at least, which by the way was the last time I worked for Henry. I was sitting at the Hotel Jerome bar about mid, then eventually late afternoon, slurping down a few cold beers, waiting for any girls to show up. This guy Bob came and sat next to me at the bar. We got to talking about goofy things we had been paid to do by rich people. Bob mentioned to me that one of his favorite stories was when some RRD, a rude rich dude, he had been doing odd jobs for wanted him to bury a white bird. No big deal, except the guy wanted him to bury the bird in some secret spot out in the forest away from everything.

I knew right away it had to be Silver. Bob told me he had finished doing some painting when the guy asked him to come in the house. The RRD had a white banker's box sitting on his desk. Bob said the guy cut through some packaging tape to open the box enough to show Bob the nearly featherless bird. Henry had frozen Silver in a plastic zip lock freezer bag, which he placed at the bottom of the banker's box. It seemed like a weird thing to do for somebody. The guy offered him two hundred bucks, way too much money for the job. Bob agreed to take the bird off the guy's hands. Of course, Bob also took the money. Bob taped the lid back on after Henry showed him the dead bird. Bob told me it seemed kind of creepy, but it was such an easy thing to do.

Bob thought I was a little crazy after I couldn't stop laughing when he told me he drove back into town right away so he could toss the box into the dumpster behind the City Market. Because, Bob told me, he figured the guy was paying him to fix some kind of drug deal that went wrong. Bob said he wasn't about to waste any time on some dumb-ass bird burying thing. I felt kind of bad talking to that Bob in the bar because when he introduced himself to me as Bob I remembered some of the awful things Silver said about various Bobs. I also felt bad because Bob was just like me. He was another guy trying to make a living by doing what he could.

So anyway that was a few months after I left Henry's employ. It was also a few months after Henry had been home when he read a story in a magazine about some guy whose bird really knew how the guy felt about things. It was after Henry read that story that I heard from him.

It happened like this. It turned out while I was still doing the house-watching Silver-feeding and listening thing, that Henry came home early from his vacation by himself. He left his wife and daughter in Chicago at her parent's house for a visit. He called me from the airport so I went to pick him up. He was back so it was time for me to leave. I packed up all my stuff in my truck then went back to the house to get paid. As he was paying me Henry smiled at me. He was polite, even courteous. He sat in his big buttery burgundy leather chair, the one I used to listen to Silver while Henry was gone. Henry cut me a check for my time. The whole time I was in the office with Henry, Silver was stone quiet as if he was dead. The bird wouldn't utter a sound. Not a peep even when Henry tried to talk to him.

So I asked him, "Hey Henry, I thought your bird could you know, talk?"

Henry looked up at me smiled then said, "You know it's the strangest thing. I've had Silver a long time, seven, almost eight years. I got him when he was pretty young, about a year old. The guy from the pet store loaned me some old cassette tapes and an old player for free so I could play the tapes that are supposed to teach a bird to talk. He said birds will say what they hear repeated to them. But, Silver, he never talks. He makes a few noises, he whistles once in a while, but not a word ever comes out of him."

"Is that right?" I said. Then I repeated like Silver did part of what Henry said. "Not a word."

"Nope, never," Henry affirmed. "About all he does is pull out his feathers when no one is around."

"Oh yeah? He does that when no one is around huh?" I said.

"I've never seen him do it," Henry said. "I thought having a bird that talked would be fun. It's not. He's been nothing but a mess."

"Too bad," I said.

I got kind of confused. Either it was true the bird never talked in front of Henry, or Henry knew all Silver did was scream like him and he didn't want me to know about it. None of which made me want to do any more work for Henry. Henry had inadvertently told me where he got the old tapes and cassette player I found in his closet.

I thanked him for the job, then I left. I cashed the check he gave me the day I got it from him. I didn't tell him my intentions were to not see him again in this life due to the fact that I believed Silver, not him. I felt a little strange putting my trust in a white cockatoo instead of its owner.

As I was leaving the house Henry walked me out to my old pickup. The thing is before I found out about Silver I had always liked Henry. I had been glad to see him, work for him. He never really did anything wrong to me that I knew of until I heard Silver. In all the screaming Silver did he had never mentioned me by name. The thing is, I was pretty sure Henry didn't know any other unnamed idiots who drove a piece of junk brown Ford Ranger with the rusty crease in the now non-opening passenger side door and grey replacement right front fender which Henry's insurance had to pay for since he had been the one who backed into it with a borrowed backhoe.

The day I left I felt rotten, relieved, and mischievous all at the same time. I felt a little guilty; because, I spent quite a bit, actually most of my paid time listening to what came out of Silver's beak. All that listening took me away from chores I could have done. But, after hearing what Silver, or I guess I should say Henry, said about those hard working people I didn't care.

I felt so angry that I didn't feel like doing any more work for Henry, no matter how much he would have paid me. I found out later that he paid lower rates than everybody else did for the same work. Which didn't surprise me after I had listened to Silver for a while.

It got to the point for me that I realized how naïve I had been. At first I thought I was mad at Henry, which I was, but then I realized it was me I had let down.

I had trusted a guy who wasn't worth trusting. I remembered various times working with the people that had done nice jobs for Henry who he complained about. He said things like it was too expensive, it took too long, and on and on and on. It was like he paid people to do things for him so he could gripe about their work. The thing is he didn't talk to them in person. He did his complaining in his office where Silver could hear him.

When I heard Henry's words coming out of Silver I realized I should have known Henry was ripping me off while he was pretending to be nice to me. He had treated me nice to my face, but when I wasn't around he was as vicious to me as he was to lots of other people who had been his "help".

After I quit working for Henry I ran into a few friends, guys I'd worked with on various jobs, who had met Henry, even some who had worked for him. Nobody had anything much good to say about him. From everyone I met who did work for him I found out that I was the only who had worked for him more than a few weeks.

The first few weeks after I stopped working for Henry he called me quite a few times. Or at least one of his secretaries did. I didn't return any of those calls. I didn't think he deserved it. I always wondered what Silver would say about that.

One time I did see Henry walking into a home improvement store. I was driving along in my old brown Ranger. I glanced at him, he caught my eye, but I kept going. In my rearview mirror he stood staring blankly at me. As I switched my view between the road ahead and my rearview mirror I was glad to see him getting smaller and smaller. I didn't stop.

I probably would have never seen him again if I hadn't seen him in court. I wondered how a guy could be like that with people. I've never really come to a good conclusion about that, not even when I got served the court papers that said I was being sued for this little story I wrote about him.

You see Henry finally found a copy of those recordings I made of Silver during my long leisurely breakfasts at his house. He was bound to find them. I recorded over the tapes Henry had used to try to teach Silver how to talk. I put the recorder and the tapes back in Henry's closet where I found them. I wasn't trying to hide them. I labelled them well. Of course I kept a couple copies of those tapes for myself in case some time in the future I felt like sharing them. Which my lawyer told me was why I won the case. On each copy of the five double-sided tapes Silver gifted me with, I put a white label on which I wrote with a black sharpie: "This is Silver telling the truth".

I changed the names, places, and faces for the magazine story. I did learn this. Even if a person's own voice doesn't sound the same to them when they hear it on a recording, each of us knows who we really are. We do recognize ourselves when we hear our own voice finally telling the truth about how we feel about ourselves and others. Sometimes we say some uplifting, encouraging, ennobling things that make people's lives better. Sometimes we don't. In court Henry testified to that.

The End

KATIE'S STORY

As she burst from below the surface of her private backyard pool, Katie blew out a large bubble of air when her chin emerged from the smooth water, which disappeared into a fine misty spray around her face and head, until the water fell around her shoulders back down into the pool. Katie stood thigh deep in the shallow end of her swimming pool. She tipped her head back as she ran both hands past her ears to gather her waist length coal black hair. She dipped her head forward then pulled her hair in front of her squeezing the water out of it with her bare hands.

"What do you want Henry?" she asked without looking at him.

Henry Brandt, her husband, squatted near the edge of the pool. He tipped up his sunglasses, then squinting against the bright Albuquerque sunlight glaring at him from the top of the pool, he looked at her with his unprotected eyes.

"Put them back on so you can see Henry," Katie told him, as she squinted at him. "The glare around the pool at this time of day is killer."

"I'm going to Seattle this morning. I won't be back until Tuesday or Wednesday," he announced.

"What are you going to do there for a week?" she wondered.

"It's going to take me that long," he explained.

"To pick up a car?"

"It won't drive itself back here," he said.

Katie put both of her arms up on the edge of the pool. She could see herself in his gold-mirrored Oakley sunglasses. She pushed herself up a little more onto the edge as she leaned toward him.

"Henry you have entirely too many cars now. What do you want with another old Kaiser? Why not have it sent?"

"Cord," he corrected her. "Totally different. I drive all my cars, you know that. They're not statues. They're made to be driven."

"Whatever," Katie said.

He stood up.

"I doubt you can stand sitting in a car for that long," she said.

"I know, I know," Henry agreed. "I can't stand sitting still that way like I used to."

She looked up at him, past him, seeing the pool house behind him. Then she focused on him. Dressed in his white K-Swiss cross trainers, brown slacks, grey belt and blue shirt.

"You're too tall for me to look at you now," she said. Then she turned her back on him so she could dive back under the water. When she came up she was standing in the center of the pool. "Besides, I want to go."

"No you don't," Henry said.

"It seems like forever when you go away like this," she complained to him. "I feel like a b-b rolling around in a bowl by myself at home, all alone."

"You know you wouldn't like it."

"I wouldn't be like last time, I promise. I wouldn't complain. I'd bring my phone, use my ear buds, I'd play my music, and read my books," Katie whined.

"Katie you know if you came you'd enjoy the flight out. And that would be all you would enjoy. After an hour in the car you'd be clawing your way through the roof to get out."

"Goodbye, so will you," she said as she slapped the water in front of her to splash him. "I'll kiss you when you come back."

Henry smiled at her, then threw her an air kiss which she pretended to catch in her right hand and place on her lips.

"I got to go. I'll miss my flight."

"Have a good time. You've got cab fare to the airport?"

"So you're not driving me?"

"My hair's wet. It'll take too long to dry. You'd be nuts by the time I was ready to go."

"I know. I already called a cab," he explained.

"Why did you even ask?"

Henry grinned at her. Turned his back to her then walked away.

She watched him walk all the way into the house. She got out of the pool to climb up onto the low diving board. She could see him in the kitchen window. She dove in the deep end swimming underwater to the shallow end. Once again she tilted her head back to blow her breath out as she surfaced. She stood up in the three foot deep water, pulled off the top and bottom of her black bikini then shook both pieces at him as he waved at her from the window. Katie could see him give his head a little shake, then he smiled again at her. Henry waved goodbye then walked away from the window so she couldn't see him anymore.

Katie got out of the pool, wrapped an oversized white towel around her body tucking it in on the sides so it would stay by itself. She went into the house to see him heading toward the front door. She quietly followed him. When she heard him close and lock the door from the outside she made her way to the front door. Through the glass window in the middle of the glossy white steel door she could see him waiting for his cab while he sat on the bench near the trees at the front of the house. She unlocked the main door so she could swing the storm door wide open to walk a few feet out of the house.

"Tuesday, maybe Wednesday?" she asked, laughing at him. Then she quickly undid her towel and threw it at him.

He jumped up to run after her. She was too quick for him. She made it into the house and locked the storm door before he could catch her.

"Goodbye Henry," she said as she pressed her naked body up against the outer glass door. He was grinning at her. Katie shook her head back and forth to tell him "no" as she pointed behind him.

"It's a trick," he said.

Then the cabbie sounded his horn.

"Cab time," she said with a big grin. She slowly closed the main inner steel door as she watched him looking at her. She could see him close his eyes and let out a big sigh as she looked at him through the little window in the door. Then she pulled the door almost closed.

She left the door open a little so she could peek at the cab as it pulled away. She watched the cab until she couldn't see it anymore. She closed the door, locked it, then she went to the master bathroom off her bedroom.

In the bathroom she looked at herself in the mirror. I look fine, not perfect, but who is she thought? As she got dressed she began wondering, now what do I do, again? I don't like going. I don't like being alone. She went out to the kitchen, turned on the oldies radio station to have some noise while she made herself a salad. She flipped pieces of lettuce, chunks of tomato, and avocado, in a big bowl, then added some raisins, chopped walnuts, pecans, broccoli and cauliflower, mixed everything all around then put it all back in the fridge without adding dressing.

Inside the fridge she noticed there wasn't any yogurt and only a little apple juice.

"I might as well go to the store," she said out loud. Even with the radio on the sound of her voice seemed to bounce off and around, the Italian porcelain tiled floor and hardwood wainscoted walls of her kitchen, for much longer than it should have. The black granite kitchen counter tops made it seem colder in the house than the thermostat reading of seventy-four degrees.

She sat up on a stool, put her feet on the rest so she could brush her long black hair. She was wearing a white sleeveless blouse, beltless stretch blue jeans, and her ruby red Rockport loafers. She liked the idea of people at the grocery store parking lot seeing her looking casual chic while getting out of her black '62 Corvette.

Pushing a grocery cart around under the fluorescent lights on that hard multi-colored commercial vinyl tiled floor that was always getting dust-mopped whenever she was in the store no matter what day or what time it was, seemed a surprisingly attractive prospect for the day. Katie was convinced that the store personnel waited to start their floor cleaning with the dust-mop until they saw or heard her pull into the parking lot in her black Corvette powered by the twin-turbocharged-five-hundred-ninety-two-cubic-inch big-block V-8 motor. She imagined them with their noses pressed to the glass windows at the front of the store watching for her to pull into the parking lot. Either that or they must dust mop all the time. It did seem incredible to her that the floor needed swept that much.

What she didn't know was the staff did dust mop when she was in the store as a way to girl watch; and, whoever was working always tried to watch her. The grocery guys did recognize the sound of her car and they very much enjoyed watching Katie wander around the store. Most of them particularly enjoyed it when unbeknownst to them she purposefully dropped on the floor, a lettuce, loose bulk items or whatever suited her fancy to give them something to clean up as well as to look at. Somehow, somewhere in the store she always hit or broke something vulnerable with her grocery cart, sometimes a display of oranges, maybe some piled up watermelon.

One time she dropped a big jar of dill pickles off the bottom rack of her cart by stopping too fast. The jar broke when it hit the hard tile floor. Pickles fell out from the broken jar as glass shards flew into the aisle. Pickle juice spread across the floor the width of the aisle. It took about two seconds for three young men in aprons and name tags to appear for the clean-up.

This day Katie had made her way through the store well enough to have collected two gallons, one of two per cent milk, and one of Tree Top apple juice as well as two quarts of plain yogurt. As she was wandering around the store she seemed to keep running into this same guy one too many times. When she emerged from the wine aisle he was once again, right in her way.

She smiled at him. Then said, "Hey you probably think I'm following you or something, but really I'm not." Then she laughed knowing it was most likely the other way around with him having been following her.

The twenty something clerk looked shocked when she spoke to him. He sheepishly looked down at the floor as he mumbled, "I'm sure you're not." He hurriedly dust-mopped away from her, careful to be sure he swept up the price tag she had knocked off the edge of the shelving with her cart.

At least she had said something to him he thought. Maybe I'll run into her again. Maybe I can talk to her again he decided as his courage increased due to her actually responding to him.

She allowed herself to notice that she thought him to be an attractive young man. He seemed nice. His long sleeve green and red plaid shirt puffed out a little past the sides of his brown canvas work apron. "Maybe not all men are perverts," she whispered softly. There he was, facing her again as she started to turn the corner around the end of the aisle.

"Did you need something?" he asked her.

"No, no I...," she started to say when he interrupted her. She turned her cart out of the way of his three-foot-wide, fringy-white dust-mop.

He pushed his dust-mop up against the end of the aisle as he leaned the handle against the shelf. "I thought I heard you say something. I didn't want to be in your way. I have to keep going around the store to get it all swept," he explained.

"Maybe you were reading my mind."

"What?" he asked her. Then he smiled widely, opening his full pink lips. The kind of lips that sometimes indicate a person who might be generous to a fault.

"Reading my mind," she explained.

"Maybe I was. What were you thinking? Will you tell me if I was right?"

"So you were trying to read my mind?"

"No. No," he said. "I was sort of following you around the store."

She smiled.

"We do that here," he said. "My co-workers and me girl watch. A lot really. And, well, if I was going to follow anyone around the store to try to get to know them it would be someone like you. I mean you're so pretty and everything. I also noticed that you have on a wedding ring which means you're married."

She nodded yes, then rotated her left hand up at him to confirm that indeed she was wearing her wedding ring.

"You're wearing a ring too," she said.

"I'm married too. My wife is in our hometown. I've been lonely for her and when I saw you I thought of her. It seems like we must have started circling around the store at about the same time in the same direction and every time I saw you I thought how pretty you are. Even after I thought I should go back the other way. I went through the whole mental game of, does she think I'm following her, she must think I'm a pervert, and I should stop following her even though I don't want to, thing? I'm sorry. Do you know what I mean?" he said. He stopped talking as his face became more and more flushed.

"Do you always talk this much to people you don't know?" she asked.

He shook his head no. Then said. "No, not really. I'm new around here. It's hard to make new real friends. I don't know anybody in the area except from the store and my church. I guess it's been a while since I had a real conversation outside work with someone besides people I'm getting to know at church."

"Yeah," she said. "I know what you mean. So what do you do?" she asked. "Away from work. Besides go to church."

"I'm a sort of gardener."

"You're a gardener?"

"That's the easy way to say I study plant physiology. I spend a lot of time in labs and greenhouses. I like it," he explained. "It's easier to say gardener than plant physiologist. It's less complicated. People understand gardener. Nobody knows what a plant physiologist does."

"You do," she said. "That's what counts. So you must be in school."

"Well sort of," he said.

"Sort of?" she asked.

"It's kind of like a private tutor kind of thing," he told her. "Hey, it looks like your milk might be getting too warm. I ought to get back to work."

"I'm keeping you from your job. You might get in trouble."

"Maybe," he said.

"Well thanks," she said. "What did you say your name was?"

"Jim, Jim, Stem."

"It's been nice meeting you Jim-Jim."

"Just Jim," he said correcting her.

"Okay, Just Jim, or Jim-Jim, which is it?" Katie said trying to make him less nervous.

"Jim Stem," he said as he held his hand out for a shake.

"Katie Brandt, with a t," she said, shaking his hand. "I've lived in this area for quite a while. Why don't you let me welcome you to town by having you over to my house sometime for a cup of coffee, or a watered down apple juice and a sandwich?"

"Mrs. Brandt I'd love to. Are you sure? I'm off work in about fifteen minutes," Jim said.

"Sounds perfect. I'm about finished here, Jim Stem, which seems like a good name for a gardener. Why don't you meet me out front in the parking lot when you're off work? I'm driving the loud black Corvette with the gold pin-striping."

"I know," he said.

Katie nodded and winked.

"My husband loves cars. He's in Seattle getting another one. The '62 Corvette is mine. I bought it myself," she paused, then said, "He did have some work done on it for me."

"Your husband is out of town?"

"Yeah, he often is," she said.

"It's nice of you to offer, but maybe I shouldn't come over if he's not home," Jim said nervously.

"Don't worry. I don't bite," she said. Then she winked at him. "It's just a sandwich."

"Okay, well sure then. I really appreciate you inviting me over to your house, although," he paused.

"Hey I'm not going to force you," Katie said. "I'm only being neighborly. Don't get the wrong idea here."

"Thank God," Jim breathed a big sigh. "I was getting kind of scared. I wasn't sure what I was getting myself into."

"Don't be nervous," she said. "You can always go home to pick up your wife. You can both come over."

"I wish I could. She's not here yet," Jim said.

"That's right you told me she's in your hometown?"

"Yeah, she's at home in Broken Arrow. That's right near Tulsa where we both grew up. I came out first to get everything set up. You know so we would have a nice place for her to come to."

"Well good. You can tell me at the house how you like Albuquerque," she said, then paused. "That is if you're coming."

"Sure. Now I only have about ten minutes more to work," Jim said.

"I'll shop some more, check out and wait in my car," Katie said. "You can follow me home."

"Seriously?"

Katie gave him a knowing smile, then said, "Sure. You do have a car don't you?"

Jim smiled back. "Yeah, I need to get this stuff put away," then he hesitated before saying. "I sure do appreciate you being nice to me."

As Katie started to walk away she waved her hand at him without turning around telling him, "See you in a few minutes."

Katie thought too bad he has to be away from his wife. I know how that feels. Katie went through the check-out line. Walked out to her car, put her stuff in on the passenger side then walked around to get into the driver's seat.

Jim could see his manager heading his way. Jim gave him a quick wave then quickly started pushing the large dust-mop toward the back of the store. His manager watched him go. Jim kept his eyes on the big white-faced black-handed store clock high up on the back wall of the store. Two minutes to two he went into the back of the store, hung up the dust mop, got his lunch box from the break room, punched out on the time clock right at two, then reappeared in the far right aisle of the store. He began to walk quickly to the front of the store to the exit that opened out into the area of the parking lot where Katie was parked.

While she was checking her car's mirrors Katie looked up. She spotted Jim coming out of the store. As he went over to his car Katie waved at him. He waved back. She pulled up next to his car so she could wave him on to follow her.

"Nice Camry," she said.

She pulled out of the lot with Jim following her and drove straight home. She parked the Corvette in the driveway, put her left arm out so she could motion Jim to pull up next to her. Then they both got out of their cars to stand in the driveway.

"I know this is a pretty cool car. It looks good. It's fun to drive. I can make a lot of smoke and noise with this car," Katie said.

"It's quite the car," Jim said.

"My husband Henry has always been a gearhead. We have a small warehouse where we, he, keeps a small collection of cars he dreamt of having since he was a kid."

"That's neat," Jim said.

"Neat?" Katie asked. "I thought neat was dry-cleaned clothes. Come on let's go in."

"Sure. Can I carry that stuff?" he asked.

"Yeah, here take the heavy stuff," Katie told him indicating the gallons of juice and milk. "You can set them on the counter in the kitchen."

While he picked up the gallons he said, "Hey thanks for having me over. I'm a little nervous, you know being new and all."

"Jim," Katie said quite seriously. "People watch too much TV and look at way too much on the net these days. I mean if you believed a tenth of what you saw on TV you'd never get out of bed in the morning."

He followed her to the door at the front of the house. She unlocked the door then motioned him to go in.

Jim went in gazing at the interior of the house.

"You have an amazing house," he said.

"Thanks," she replied. "You can set the groceries there on the counter."

"Oh, yeah," Jim responded.

Katie held up a coffee mug she pointed in Jim's direction that had a picture of a red and black Duesenberg on it. "Regular or unleaded?"

"Regular, milk and sugar."

"So tell me why you're in town. When your wife is coming to be with you. All that stuff. Don't worry I'm not a gossip. I'm not going to tell anyone about you. I've lived here long enough to know better. But, don't be surprised when you get some strange looks from people back at the market."

Jim wandered out of the kitchen toward the living room. He noticed a glass cabinet filled with trophies from martial arts competitions. He saw trophies inscribed with Katie's name on them.

"Hey Jim," she said a bit more loudly than necessary. "I'm only being a good neighbor inviting you here. I didn't invite you here for any funny business. So don't get any crazy ideas about me. I can handle myself."

Jim put his palms in the air. "Okay, no problem. I can leave now if you want. I only agreed to come because you asked me."

"I'm sorry. I didn't mean to yell at you. I'm a little nervous too," Katie said. "I hope you're not some kind of kook or something."

"Na," Jim said. "I'm just me. Trying to earn enough money to get my wife out here so we can be together. I probably shouldn't be here. It's just that in the store us guys talk about meeting some of the women who come in the store so when you talked to me. It was like a dream come true."

"A dream?"

"Yeah, like it wasn't real you even spoke to me."

"I'm real," Katie said.

"I know. That's what makes it so like a dream. I never thought I'd be going to someone's home except my own. I mean you're a customer at the market."

"I know," Katie said. "I thought the same thing. You seemed nice to talk to. I didn't see the harm in talking to you a little more. Especially when we had a nice chat at the store."

"Okay, well, uh, I was looking at the trophies in the other room," Jim said. "Are they all yours?"

"Yeah, I was into martial arts for a long time. Not so much in the last couple of years. I used to say it keeps me in shape and Henry in line," She said.

"Oh!" he said.

"That's a joke," she explained. "I'm a little angry at my husband today. He went out of town this morning to get another car," Katie said. "Here's your coffee."

"Thanks. I sure miss my wife. We've never been apart before this. We've only been married three years. We have a two-year-old daughter. Her name is Melissa. Here, I can show you her picture. I have some in my wallet," Jim said as he reached into his back pocket to extract his family pictures.

"So it really is true?" Katie asked.

"True?"

"Well, that parents still carry pictures of their children with them," Katie said.

Jim smiled at Katie as he laid out pictures of his wife and daughter on the black granite. "I know huh? Most people whip out their phone to show you all their pictures. I probably would too if I had a phone like that. All I've got is a couple paper pictures."

"Your wife has a name?" Katie prodded.

"Tina, my wife," Jim told her as he pointed to each person in the photo. "This is Melissa, she's two."

"I think it's great you have pictures with you all the time. So tell me when your wife will be coming to be with you?"

"It's not that complicated really. She has a job as a nurse. At one time I wanted to be a medical doctor. The only problem was I can't stand the sight of blood. I pass out."

Katie smiled widely at Jim. "No kidding? I promise I won't cut myself while you're here. So what are you doing working at the market? Can't you get a gardening job here?"

"I needed the money. I'm working on my doctorate doing research for my dissertation. What I do is pretty high tech gardening."

"Good for you Jim," she said. "I feel better about inviting you here. You must be pretty smart in science. I haven't had science since high school which was a few years ago."

"Not into science huh?"

"Not so much."

"How about you? Do you have any children?"

"No we don't have any. Henry likes cars. We haven't really talked about it much. We have each other. Nobody else. My parents died when I was young. They left me a lot of money. Henry was a foster kid as a little guy then all on his own after about sixteen. We get along really well. Probably because we both grew up mostly alone. Maybe that's why we don't have kids."

"Kids take a lot of time and attention," Jim said. "I really miss my family. It's only temporary though. They are the most important part of my life. Along with my faith."

"Oh? Right, you're a religious person aren't you?" Katie said.

"Yeah, I would say so. I don't go around with a sign on my forehead. I guess I believe more in living it out, trying to be a good example instead of talking people into something like some kind of salesman."

"Oh yeah? Do you think sometimes people want you to talk about God to them? I mean they could be waiting, maybe begging for someone to talk about God, or at least something spiritual to them?" Katie proposed.

"Yeah, well I guess sometimes. I think it's a little tricky. I mean I felt like it was okay for me to come here today. So I came. I wouldn't have come if I felt too uncomfortable," Jim said.

Katie felt a kind of quietness about her. "Well I'm glad you came Jim. Maybe you can tell me more about why I invited you. This isn't what I do. I have never invited a complete stranger, especially a man, into my home even when my husband was here. Maybe you need to tell me why you accepted my invitation," Katie told him.

"I thought you said you did this all the time?" Jim asked.

"I lied, a little. I didn't think you would accept. But, here you are."

"Maybe I should go," he said.

"No don't go," Katie said. "I mean you're here now," she went on to say, as she thought to herself, he must be thinking I'm some kind of pervert or something. "Really it's okay. I guess I was feeling a little strange today. A little lonely with my husband gone again. I had a feeling about you, a good feeling. I mean I felt good about talking to you. You don't scare me or anything. I can take care of myself, but I mean I felt comfortable with you. Listen to me, I'm talking to you like we're old friends."

They smiled at one another. Then they each took a deep breath, sighing in relief at what Katie said.

She shuffled a few loose items around on the kitchen counter to dispel some of the embarrassment she felt after her candid explanation.

"Maybe you could tell me a little more about yourself," she said. "So you're a kind of plant doctor, you're married, and you have a daughter. You don't seem very religious. I mean you seem like lots of other people I know."

Jim smiled. "I suppose I do. I mean, I'm sure I'm like other people. I'm not any different than other people."

"It seems like everybody I know isn't religious, but they do the same kinds of things you do."

"Well like I said. To me being a believer is a daily lived out thing. To me religion is how a person lives out what they believe. Not just a person telling everybody in words what they say they believe."

"Like putting your money where your mouth is?" Katie asked.

"Yeah, pretty much. You could say that."

"So do you belong to a church?"

"Yeah, I'm Roman Catholic."

"No kidding? What about all those pervert priests that were in the news all the time?" Katie asked.

Jim glanced at the floor then looked up into Katie's eyes. "That's been a big problem for sure. In reality it has only been a small proportion of bad apples giving the rest a bad name. I can't make any excuses for that kind of behavior. I know it cuts into the credibility of the church for some people. For me the bottom line is the message of Jesus, which is that everybody is capable of loving. We all need help to live day to day. Some of us get into trouble and need more help than others. It's like those football games where people in the stadiums held up scripture passages saying 'God so loved the world He sent his son into the world to save it not to condemn it'. To me that scandal stuff is exactly the kind of thing that God wants to save us from. Sexual excesses, drugs, alcohol, things that really hurt us. Salvation isn't simply a pie in the sky kind of a thing. It's meant to start now and continue after this life in to resurrected life. Everybody is redeemable, even if they don't know what it means."

"That's a way of looking at it I hadn't ever heard of before Jim," Katie told him. "You sound like you've thought a lot about this stuff."

"I've had to I guess. I mean as a believer I can't ignore what has gone on in the name of what I believe in. I mean lots of people have problems with what they call institutional churches. If you think about it institutions are people. Its people who make them go. They are there to help us live out our spiritual life. There isn't anything more wrong with institutions than there is wrong with the people running them."

While Jim was talking Katie began to think about her life. What do I believe in? I have always believed in God. Well at least that there was one. What Jim is saying makes a lot of sense. There seems to be so much to it.

"Why does it always sound like some complicated game?" Katie said out loud realizing she had drifted from her and Jim's conversation to her own thoughts.

"It's not a game. Everything we do counts. All the time, every time," Jim said.

"Like the butterfly effect?" Katie asked.

"From Ray Bradbury's story, 'A sound of Thunder'?" Jim said.

"I don't know. I never read that. I only heard people refer to the butterfly effect as something little that influences everything else," Katie said.

"I think that's a good way to put it. There are more and more people realizing not only does everything we do affect everybody else in some way. It also means that we are part of a big family. The human family that has disagreements, longings, all on a planet wide scale. I don't think people are fundamentally different. We all want what we think is best for ourselves. Things get messed up when the desires of people don't line up. People believe different things even inside their own religions. All you have to do is look at wars that have been fought with each side believing God was on their side. The warring parties must have had different perceptions of who God is. The "Ten Commandments" tell us to not fight with our family. As humans we are starting to realize we're all related, which makes us all members of the human family. So why should we be fighting with each other?"

"You make it sound so simple."

"I think the most important things are simple. Everybody understands them. Not everyone needs to have some advanced degree in theology to know that love is the most important thing people can do. Our human nature is to love. We even love things that are bad for us. We hurt ourselves in the deepest aspect of our nature by doing things to hurt ourselves."

"I think everybody knows that one. I certainly do."

"Yeah, we've all loved people or things in the wrong way. The thing is we did love them. We don't do things to ourselves because we hate ourselves. We do things in our self-interest because we love ourselves. The trick is to learn how to seek the good of other people. We live on a planet wide school of love. Long before there was all the various Christian denominations around today, there was a monk named St. Benedict who lived around the sixth century. He wrote a rule, based on the gospel, for monks, which said the monastery was a school of love. The idea was to go to a monastery to learn how to love people. When a person learned how to do that in their own monastic family it was thought they would leave monastic life to go live in the world which needed to be loved."

"Really? I thought monks wanted to get away from everybody."

"Yeah, I suppose some of them do, for a while. Monks are like everybody else. They're only people who live in a monastery."

"So how long does it take to learn how to love?" Katie asked.

Jim smiled at Katie.

"So what are you smiling about?" She said.

"How long do you think it takes someone to learn how to love?" Jim asked.

"I'm not sure."

"You love your husband right?"

"Of course."

"The same as always?"

Katie smiled then said, "I know I love him differently than I used to. We've been together quite a while."

Jim nodded.

"There's a comfort and security in our relationship now that hasn't always been there. I know Henry loves me. He knows I love him. We trust each other."

"The better your married love is the more it allows you to love other people."

"I think you're right. How do you know all this stuff? You're still a kid."

"I learned it from other people. It's the teaching of my church. Before we got married Tina and I had to take a class about what it means to get married in the church. That's where we both learned about this stuff. Everybody who gets married in the church learns it. It's required to know before the priest will allow you to get married in the church. A person doesn't have to know it perfectly, but we're taught it. Marriage in the church is supposed to be for the enhancement of the whole community not only for the two people marrying each other. We get married to each other as members of the greater community so we can be better members of our community too."

"It sounds so, for lack of a better way to put it, good," she said.

"It is good. I think a lot of people don't know how good it is. I mean lots do. They live it as best they can. There are a lot of people who never heard of most of the things in the church that are really good for them."

"Yeah?" Katie asked.

"I think if more people knew of the good things in the Catholic Church than a lot of the bad press they do hear they might see a lot of things from a different perspective that could help them when they needed it."

Katie nodded, then said, "Yeah maybe."

"I've finished off the coffee you gave me. I probably ought to be getting home."

"Don't you want a sandwich?"

"I do, but I've been here a while. I don't want to overstay my welcome. I think I ought to be going," Jim said.

Katie nodded again.

"Yeah, okay that might be a good idea. I'll see you in the store again sometime," Katie said.

"Yeah, I have to keep working there to keep myself in school. I save as much as I can these days. Like I said I don't even have my own phone right now." Jim said as he gave Katie a big smile.

She turned to Jim as she smiled at him too. Her smile was a small, sad little smile that she wished she could have hidden. It seemed obvious to her that her guest could see how embarrassed she was. Or maybe not. How would he know whether or not her sadness was simple loneliness or something else? After all, to her he was such a kid.

"It's been great to have you here Jim. I'm glad you agreed to at least have some coffee with me."

"Thanks. I miss my wife. I can imagine what the guys at the store are going to say to me. I mean the fact that I left work about the same time you left means they will be making up some kind of nonsense fantasy to tease me about."

"I can imagine."

"So. I guess I need to be going Mrs. Brandt."

"Okay then," she said.

As Katie walked Jim out toward the front door she said, "I'll let you out. I'll see you in the store."

As he walked along behind her he said, "I go to Our Lady of Guadalupe Catholic church. It's not far from here actually. It's over on Griegos Road NW." Jim said.

"I know where that is," Katie said. "I've driven past it a few times."

"Maybe you could come to church there sometime. I try to always get there on Sunday at ten. Sometimes my store schedule has me lined up to work Sunday morning. So I go Saturday evening to the vigil mass at 5:30 pm. I don't have to be there for you to go to church. There's lots of really nice people there."

Jim kept talking as they walked toward the front door. "Thanks a lot for the coffee. We always have coffee and treats after Sunday mass. If you ever decide to come to church that would be great. I feel better now that I know it's okay to talk to you in the store. If you ever want to talk some other time you can always reach me through the church, or come into the store. When I can I go to mass during the week too, at nine am."

"Okay," she said. "Thanks for letting me know," Katie told him as she opened the door to let him out.

Katie gave Jim a wan smile. She watched him through the glass storm door as he walked down the driveway to his car.

"Coffee and treats. Not exactly what I need to make Henry happy," she said as she patted herself on her firm muscular belly.

Katie slowly closed the inner door. She didn't watch Jim drive away. In silence she made her way into the bathroom. After tinkling she went into the living room where she slumped into Henry's favorite luxurious leather reclining chair. For the next two days, Wednesday and Thursday, Katie binge watched from the internet. She watched shows she liked, some she didn't. She was the proverbial b-b in a bowl rolling around aimlessly for two days until her phone rang at nine-thirty Thursday night. She was making her way back into the living room with a tuna sandwich, barbeque potato chips, and iced lemonade. She set the tray down, then while still standing she answered the cordless house phone.

"Yes," she said.

"Hello ma'am. This is the Utah state police. My name is Officer Duane Young. Am I speaking to Mrs. Kathleen Brandt?"

"Yes, I'm Mrs. Brandt," she said.

"Mrs. Brandt I'm sorry I have some bad news for you. You might want to be sitting down."

"Why should I sit down?" Katie said. "Why are you calling me?"

"I'm sorry ma'am, I'm calling to inform you that your husband Henry Brandt was involved in a fatal traffic accident late this afternoon."

She dropped the wireless phone. It kept talking to her from the floor.

"Ma'am? Ma'am? Can you hear me?"

Katie sat down on the floor near where the phone fell next to Henry's chair.

The phone was louder as she sat next to the receiver.

"Ma'am, are you all right?"

Katie picked up the phone.

"Do you think I'm all right officer when everything is all wrong?"

"I'm so sorry to have to call you with this information Mrs. Brandt. Do you have someone you can talk to, a friend, pastor or someone like that I can contact for you?"

"No," Katie said. "Can you tell me what happened?"

"Yes," he said. "Your husband was driving his car on a quiet two lane highway heading southeast, when it appears he experienced a blowout. The car swerved off into a ditch, then turned over. Your husband was ejected from the vehicle. From all we can tell he never suffered. We found the accident site after a trucker called it in on his cell phone. I was the first officer on the scene so I know first-hand what happened."

"Thank you officer. Was he alone?"

"There is no evidence that there was anyone else in the car."

"So it was him and the car?"

"Yes ma'am. I have a phone number you can call if you feel the need to talk to someone. I'm calling to let you know you'll have to come here to take care of the legal part of things. To tie up loose ends."

"I have to go there?"

"Yes ma'am. Your husband's body was taken to the closest funeral home which is in Price, Utah. You will need to go there to take care of things regarding the disposition of your husband's body. I don't imagine you want to talk about the situation with the car he was driving; however, at some time you'll need to deal with the car itself."

"Yes, I understand," Katie said. "Thank you for calling."

"Mrs. Brandt please call me if there is anything I can do for you, anything at all."

"Thank you Duane. I know how to get help if I need to. I will be coming to Utah right away to take care of my husband."

"My thoughts and prayers are with you tonight Mrs. Brandt."

"Yeah, okay, Officer."

Katie set the wireless handset on the receiver. Then she went into her bedroom, pressed her face into Henry's pillows, and cried herself to sleep.

Katie woke up pre-dawn. She watched the first sunlight creep its way through her curtains. The house was the same as when she went to bed. TV was on, her food untouched on the tray. She left it that way as she got ready to go to Utah. It took her a little less than two weeks to take care of everything.

When she got home her two week old tray full of sandwich, chips and lemonade was the first thing she threw away. She turned off the TV. She couldn't get herself to sit in Henry's chair. She lay down on the couch in the quiet of her home with the relentless realization that Henry was never coming back. Death was so final seemed like such a trite thing to say to yourself. It was the day to day grief that washed over her in waves she couldn't control that hit her hardest. It would be like when she fell off her board surfing. While the same wave that knocked her over pummeled her into the sand on the bottom, it would hold her there, making her feel completely helpless until the entire ocean decided to let her up for air.

Katie knew she had to do something for herself. The grief she endured while she was awake invaded her dreams. She had dreams where she was trapped in a basement or in a room filling with water from which her only escape was to wake up. When she woke scared from those dreams she was sweating, and breathing hard. It wasn't long before she was afraid to sleep. When she was awakened in the night she would feel compelled to get out of bed. The only way Katie knew to escape from her dreams was to run away from them. She would walk around the house, turn the TV on. She tried listening to loud music.

Once she went for a drive in her Corvette still dressed in her nightie, but the car, the driving, so strongly reminded her of Henry she had to pull off to the side of the road to cry. Katie's crying didn't seem to help her. Her fits of nearly uncontrollable sobbing came with gasps for breath and sighs so deep from inside of her she was afraid she might burst. She had lost her ability to make herself laugh. No longer could she use her intelligent sarcasm to rescue her from things which she had always thought were beneath her. Katie had never known such severe vulnerability.

She had always been so strong. She used to miss Henry when he would go on trips. Now that he was gone, the fact that she was alone in the world, which had only been a vague notion in the back of her mind until it actually happened, devastated her.

In the more than three weeks since she had been back from burying Henry in Utah she had only been out of her house the night she took the Corvette for a late night drive. She was running out of food. She needed to do something besides grieve. She alternated between various emotional highs and lows. Katie couldn't believe Henry was gone. She was angry at him for leaving her, wanted him back, but knew she couldn't have that. Katie was alone in the world. She didn't want to be alone anymore.

She examined herself in the mirror. "Not that bad, really," she told herself. "A little shampoo, a shower, I'll be good to go."

By the time she ended up parked in the lot at her usual grocery store, she had to take a few deep breaths to go in. There had been entirely too many people to negotiate in traffic. Now she would have to actually talk to people without having the luxury of a phone between herself and them. Then she remembered to shut off the Corvette. She almost got out with it still idling in neutral. She almost laughed at herself. She put on the parking brake, put the transmission in reverse, made sure the windows were up. One last check in her mirror, then she got out.

Katie walked quietly from her car to the front door of the store. She had on a pair of comfortable cross trainers, a pair of her black stretch jeans, a light blue blouse and a medium sized straw hat from which she could look at people then drop the hat brim so they couldn't see her.

The sound of the store's double door hissing open gave her a start. Her hands were sweating when she grabbed hold of the grocery cart handle. The handle felt real, reassuring, it was solid in her hands. It was something hard she could hold onto without herself or anyone else knowing that's what she needed to do in this public place.

Katie looked as beautiful as ever. It wasn't long before some grocer was sweeping the already swept aisles or facing the shelves in aisles where she lingered. She didn't know what to buy. For weeks she hadn't felt like eating much anyway. All the cans looked pretty much the same to her. She found herself smiling a little as she noticed how many different colored cans of beans were available. There were so many different choices of green beans, then there were the red beans, black beans, white beans, yellow beans, so many that, she decided to not buy any beans at all. Then she noticed out of the corner of her eye, as she looked from beneath the rim of her hat, the edge of a wide dust mop moving lazily around near the end of the aisle at the front part of the store.

Katie lifted her head to see that there was indeed a young man pushing a half-aisle-wide dust-mop around near the front of the store. He looked directly at her matching her gaze. He smiled at her. She frowned at him then rolled her eyes dramatically as she lowered the brim of her hat. She slowly shook her head back and forth. The young man laughed at her. A manager walked up to the young man, said something to him that Katie couldn't have cared less about hearing or knowing. All she really wanted was some fresh fruit, perhaps some fish if it looked good. That young man had been so rude to her. He had been no Jim.

"I know I wanted something to eat, but did I come back to this place so I could talk to Jim?" she asked herself out loud.

"What did you say?" a woman near her asked. "Were you talking to me young lady?"

Katie, who it seemed had not heard the woman, shook her head to indicate no as she started pushing her cart toward the produce section of the store. The store's produce man for the day, who looked to be at least fifty years old, was cutting and dropping leaves from cauliflowers into a forest green thirty-three gallon garbage can. When he approved of how they looked he placed the trimmed white cauliflowers next to one another in neat rows of the refrigerated produce display case. As Katie approached the area where the man was working she stopped about ten feet behind him. She watched him cut cauliflower for what seemed to her quite a long time.

As the produce man looked back and forth across his display case he noticed Katie standing quietly behind him. He turned toward her. "Can I help you?" he asked.

She squinted at him. He was clearly not Jim either.

"Do you know a Jim that works here?"

"Which one?"

"The chemist, plant scientist, Catholic one," Katie said.

"Yeah, I remember him. He doesn't work here anymore. Are you like a friend of his or something?"

"Yeah, a friend. A really good friend."

The produce man grinned at her. "Lucky Jim, we call him around here," he said.

"Lucky Jim?" Katie asked.

"Nothing, yeah, well anyway he had some kind of family emergency or something and left about two or three weeks ago. That's all I know. Maybe you can talk to the manager. She might be able to help you. Want to buy some cauliflower?"

Katie shook her head no. Then she walked away leaving her cart sitting where she had stopped to watch the produce guy.

"Bye," he said.

Katie ignored him. On her way out of the store she bought a half gallon of ready to drink orange juice and a box of soda crackers.

When she got in her car she kept the windows up until she was sweating. She watched people come and go from the store and the parking lot while she ate crackers from the box and drank juice from the jug. She dropped crumbs on her blouse and pants. After she had eaten enough crackers Katie put the open box on the floor on the passenger side. Then she swigged down about a third of the orange juice in three big gulps before she screwed the black lid back on the jug. The orange juice made her burp. Not burp, belch. Katie belched then she laughed. She rolled the driver side window down to try to cool off. Then she noticed a young man carrying a skateboard under his left arm was passing by on the driver side of her car. He was giving her a thumbs up sign.

"Cool car," he said. Then he smiled at her.

She saw him smiling at her so she smiled back and said, "Thanks."

Then Katie smelled a strong odor of marijuana. She began laughing a little.

The young man started laughing with her.

She laughed a little louder when she realized the young man was stoned. Then she kept laughing because it felt good.

The young man kept walking toward the store.

"I can't remember the last time I did that," Katie said.

Katie wiped a few tears off her cheeks. She started the Corvette with a vengeance. She revved it up loud, for about two seconds to listen to the sound it could make. She looked around to see if people were looking at her. The young stoned man who was on the sidewalk in front of the store held his skateboard high in the air with his left hand while at the same time he pumped his right fist in the air. He was nodding his head allowing his long hair to swing freely.

"Yeah, baby, let her rip," he yelled.

"That was fun. I haven't had any fun for too long."

On her way out of the parking lot Katie drove as quietly and safely as she could. She stopped in front of the store where the young man with the skateboard was watching her drive. Katie waited patiently for a lady escorting an older woman, who was probably the lady's mom, into the store so they could go shopping. The two women walked right in front of Katie's idling Corvette. Katie reached her left hand out the window to give the young man with the skateboard a big thumbs up.

"Hey, kid." Katie said.

"Yeah?" the young man answered.
"Don't go in the store for a minute, okay?"
"Sure," he said.
"Okay, this won't take long," she said.

Katie made her way to the street in first gear. She maneuvered her slow moving car into the middle of the right lane then she jammed her accelerator pedal to the floor.

If they had been listening closely which one young man in front of the store was doing, people around the area of the store could have heard, for a split second, the twin turbochargers Henry had installed on the highly-modified-five-hundred-ninety-two-cubic-inch-big-block Chevy V-8 sucking in huge amounts of air, before they heard the deafening sound of exhaust and burning tires.

All that air mixing with all that fuel made it possible for the twelve-hundred-fifty-horsepower motor to send enough power to the rear wheels to make the car leap forward. Katie didn't want to make the car leap forward. She didn't even want to go fast. She wanted to make herself feel good by pushing her car hard. Katie's Corvette churned out a deafening ground-pounding mixture of thundering exhaust and burning tires that made most of the people near-by cover their ears. The rear tires of the Corvette went up in smoke for more than fifty feet until Katie didn't want that to happen anymore.

She hadn't gained much speed while the tires were burning off a large cloud of rancid blue smoke. Inside the car Katie had been screaming as loud as she could, "Go, Go, Go," until she decided not to. She stopped the massive noise making event when she felt like it. It was only a matter of seconds. When she was finished screaming and burning up her tires Katie drove twenty five miles an hour in the direction of Griegos Road NW to find her friend Jim. She kept her Corvette at twenty five, five miles an hour under the thirty mile an hour speed limit.

On the way she said, "Thank you Henry for making that kind of thing possible for me to do. That really helped, but that's not enough. I need to do more than spin my wheels for the rest of my life. Henry no matter what happens from now on. I will always love you."

The End

MOTOR TERRY

Terry could see a light rain had fallen as he surveyed the terrain in front of him. The bottom of the hill was only about fifty or sixty feet below and the ruts didn't look bad enough to affect his steering. The area was new to him, but he decided to try it anyway. His new motocross motorcycle was a two hundred fifty cc two-cycle Husqvarna. He had been riding it for a few months getting pretty well used to it. From the top of the hill he could see a small gully sloping down from the road to the right as well as a shoulder of rocks curving off to the left. At the bottom of the hill the road flattened out next to the edge of the field it bordered. He could see the town of Era in the distance lit by sun light filtering through the clouds.

He stopped sightseeing and gunned it down the hill. He hit a rut. It turned the front wheel sideways to the left, the ground was slippery clay. The rut was far deeper than he thought. He tried to power out of it only his front wheel was turned too far beneath him to recover an upright position. The front wheel slid sideways into the bottom of the rut causing the rear end of the bike to buck up into the air. He pitched forward from the seat while he tried to keep from flying over the handlebars by pushing hard on the handgrips with both arms. The pressure was too much. The back end of the motorcycle swung around as it pitched forward. As the front end was switching places with the back end the bike was sideways in the road. Terry was out of control. He pulled violently on the left side of the handlebar in a desperate effort to straighten out the bike. It had come too far around.

The angle of the hill was too great for him to keep from crashing. The right handlebar hit first. It dug into the muddy clay. The right foot-peg hit next then the rider's leg touched the ground. Together he and the bike slammed into the greasy clay dirt until his foot became pinned between the engine case and the ground. His helmeted head banged into the ground then bounced off to bang again. He raised his right arm from the right handlebar to protect his head. He held onto the left handlebar trying to pull the clutch lever so the bike wouldn't dig itself into the ground with its back wheel. Then he pushed the kill switch.

His collar was full of mushy, chunky, grayish-colored clay mud. His right foot felt broken inside his boot that was still pinned under the bike. His gloved hands were unbroken, but sore. He wasn't unconscious. The first thought he had was to get his foot out from under his bike. Then, he began to think. I'm not too far from my van, and the first time I go riding by myself I crash.

Except for the pain shooting up his right leg he felt fine. He lay panting as he rested a few minutes before moving anything except his hands. It hurt too much to move. He thought he had screamed. The middle of the week in a new place with nobody else around.

He looked his bike over while he lay in the slimy dirt. He could see the handlebar was bent, the brake lever was bent. Even so the bike looked rideable. It looked like he made it about halfway down the hill. His foot hurt like hell.

It started to rain again. He took his helmet off then turned over onto his back. He knew his rain gear would keep him dry enough. He smelled fuel, but was overcome with pain and passed out.

He hurt, felt tired and hadn't figured on falling asleep. His head was dripping wet when he woke. He could still smell fuel. The rain water was running down the hill off him and his motorcycle. He was close enough to reach the toolkit he had added to the handlebar. He opened the kit for access to the tools so he could take off the handlebar. He used the handlebar to lever his foot out from under the bike and as a cane to push himself up into a crouching position. Terry rested a while soaking up the pain. He noticed when he had the bike levered up a little to pull his foot from under the engine case that the bike had stopped sliding because the gas tank caught on a rock. He stood on his left leg using both hands on the handlebar cane for balance. The new rain was making the ground slicker and slicker while it exposed rocks near the surface.

He figured his van to be no farther than three miles away. He would only have to follow the road to be safe. The van was an automatic. He could drive with a lame leg to the town hospital. The hill would be the hardest part. It wasn't the longest, or steepest terrain he had ridden all day, it was the slickest.

For the most part the area around the town of Era was low rolling hills of dirt and sage brush. Some of the fire roads were accessible by car. Motorcyclists moved in a few years back in increasing numbers to crowd up the whole county on weekends. The federal government owned the land and riders went where they wanted to. Farm boys from around Era drove their trucks out in the hills for pleasure as well as to watch the weekend motorcyclists ride up and down the hills like porpoises surfacing and diving disappearing and reappearing. Today no one had been there to see Terry race down the hill out of sight, alone.

Using the handlebar cane to balance with his left arm he could pull his right leg with his right arm to force himself up the hill.

The bottom of his riding boots were not only clogged with the sticky clay soil, every step he took added more of the sticky stuff. The dirt was like greasy glue. He slipped and slid in the clay as he tried to make his way uphill. He had more and more trouble dragging his leg because both his feet were getting heavier with every step from the clay adding itself to his boots.

Terry had been trucking around the state trying to improve enough to turn pro next season. He was in excellent physical shape, twenty two years old, prime age to make the change to pro. He could get a big money sponsor next year and have it made.

Then he slipped and fell. His head hurt. He fell on his front then turned over on his back. With his helmet off his head was soaked. Water ran down inside his jacket. His face reflected the agony of broken bones as well as being alone in the open on foot.

For a while the water on his back felt good. Then it turned cold. He looked uphill. He thought if he could get up over the rise he might be able to see his van. He was no more than forty feet from the top. He stood up as straight as he could. The blood drained from his head. He fainted, fell again. The jolt of hitting the ground forced him into awareness. He tried to clear his head thinking, how stupid! All I have to do is put the handlebar back on the bike to ride out of here.

He pushed himself on his rump to slide down the slick gooey clay hill to the bike. He put the bar back on the upper triple clamp, swung the bike around on its side facing it the right direction for him to get back on. He saw the angle of the hill, figured the best way to use the bike's own weight to leverage it into an upright position.

His bare head ached now, his eyes were blurring. Thinking it must be the rain in his eyes he positioned himself under the bike for the push. He sat side-saddle, pushed with his left leg and arm. He kept smelling fuel. The bike went up slowly, but it wasn't enough. He set it back down. He miscalculated the angle. Terry moved the bike so it was nose down the hill a bit. He figured if he got it moving this time he could hop on, head down-hill into the bottom of the gully to start the bike in motion, turn around, head back up-hill having an easy ride back to the van.

He angled the front wheel down-hill, pushed the bike up with his left leg as he held his right broken foot as still as he could by forcing his knee into the gas tank. Pushing on the right handle bar as well as pushing up with his left leg made the bike stand up. He had put it in second gear to be ready for a bump start. He got rolling fast enough for him to dump the clutch. The rear wheel slid, spun a little, slid some more, then spun a little faster, enough for the bike to fire right up. He pulled in the clutch to get the motor warmed up.

It had been a good thing he had come out early today. It was still before noon on his watch. He had plenty of time to take it slow in the van all the way back to Era long before sundown. At the bottom of the hill he waited a few moments throttling up the bike. He looked out past the town of Era at sunlight piercing the overcast rainclouds in the far distance near the horizon. Terry smiled as best he could. Seeing the sunlight made him feel warmer.

He pointed the bike straight up the hill, put it in low gear, not wanting to take any chances of it losing power or going too fast in the mud. He didn't want to washout again. He went fifteen feet and knew he would be able to make it. Then as he pushed his knee firmly against the fuel tank he noticed a crack in the top of the tank. That's where the fuel smell was coming from, but he couldn't stop now. The engine was more than strong enough. He shifted to second to keep from bogging down in the muck. After forty five feet he knew he had it made. Then the engine chugged, coughed, the bike lurched, more throttle made it cough worse. It slowed. Terry panicked.

He though it couldn't be out of fuel! Something else had to be wrong. Maybe the tank leaked when it was lying on its side. There could be water in the fuel. The bike had been getting as wet as he was. Maybe it was too wet to run. Terry locked up the front wheel with the front brake so he could set the bike down on its left side. He put his left leg over the tank thinking he could land sidesaddle on the seat flat on his back, both legs on the bike's right side. He flopped down hard onto his back. He hit his head on an exposed rock. His arms lay loosely on the ground. His right hand was on the seat a bit behind him. His left leg and hand were near the handlebar. He lay limp, unmoving, as rain fell gently on the hillside where he lay.

Jack and Tim Logan got the afternoon off from the warehouse where they worked, packed up a case of beer and headed out to the hills. Jack drove a new Dodge Ram pickup that he had recently finished breaking in. He had it lifted at the local Les Schwab's so the oversized wheels and thirty-six inch dirt tires he wanted on it would fit. He wanted to see what it would do in what he knew from the recent rain would be slimy, greasy clay mud.

The two of them came upon Terry's van. They decided to follow the same trail Terry had taken. "Some punks out here racing around again. Kind of late or kind of early depending on your point of view huh Tim?" Jack said with a beer laugh.

"Let's outdo them in your new truck," Tim said trying to coax Jack into gunning his truck around.

They followed Terry's track as well as they could in the mud. It rained a lot that day. Jack let off the gas a little to stop from spraying mud so he could look over the top of the same hill Terry stopped at earlier in the day. Jack stopped short of the edge to look out over the valley. He turned off his motor to listen.

Tim said, "Those guys are sure quiet today."

"Maybe they took off back to where they came from on their bikes."

Jack was feeling pretty good. Not hearing the giant mosquito kind of whine that some of the two-cycle motorcycles made was fine to him.

After sitting long enough to finish off another beer, Jack started the truck. Then he edged it over the top to get a straight shot at the steep hill he knew was on the other side of his truck-hood-obscured view.

The truck had barely crested the ridge when Jack jerked Tim into the dash by slamming the brakes hard. The new tires bit into the slick clay bringing the truck to a quick stop.

"You see him?" Tim said.

"Yeah that's why I stopped," Jack replied.

Tim hopped out of the truck. He reached Terry first, with Jack right behind him.

"He looks like he's out cold," Tim said.

Jack bent over Terry. "He ain't breathing."

"He's dead?" Tim asked.

Jack nodded his head. "Looks like," Jack said.

The two of them picked Terry up from where he lay on his back. They took him to the hospital in Era where the doctor told them he had died of a combination of things. The guy had more than one severe knock to the head, internal bleeding with cracked and broken ribs, as well as a broken right foot and ankle.

By the time they left the hospital Jack had sobered up quite a bit. On their way out of the hospital Tim had another question for Jack.

"Hey, why do you think he was out there all alone Jack?"

Jack shrugged his shoulders. Then he put his hands in his pants pockets as he walked back to his new truck.

The End

THE OLD MAN

Nestled on the edge of a plywood plant near an industrial railroad crossing squats a plywood shanty. From its top spouts a stovepipe, puffing small clouds of wood smoke gently into billows of smog surrounding the plant. For about fifteen years the Unico wood products corporation has owned the property where the shanty sits. Unico seems as yet unable to use the area. It is non-agricultural, but not too rocky for a small garden. There is usually a dog or two, sometimes more lazing around the place. At least they seem to be lazy when they are by the shack.

At five o'clock in the morning a stooping short-gaited man emerges from the shanty with a bowl of food for dogs. He cautiously bends over setting the food in little piles amidst licking, hungry animals of all sizes making sure each gets his or her fair share. Breakfast is unhurried. The old man sits on a wooden apple box and watches them, waiting until they are finished. Some eat more than others and those finishing before the rest are welcomed by him for mutual affections.

It is still early. The sun is growing for the day. Quiet has not yet been destroyed by progress at the plant.

Sunday, Christmas, and Thanksgiving Day are the only days the workers stay home. Most of them are unskilled and their work makes them resemble robots in action. Tasks at the plant linger in the gray area between being too complicated for machines and too easy for people. A person can function well enough to do their work even if they're half asleep or hung-over.

Business begins at six a.m. and ends at five p.m. A steam whistle blows three times a day. To begin, to eat and to end. The whole operation is less than sixteen years old. When the corporation bought the property they didn't bother to fence it or post no trespassing signs. Since the railroad was so close road kings and wayfarers moved in.

A small river with plenty of trout bordered the plant on one side opposite the town, the railroad on another and some lines on a map in the courthouse decided the other two.

The plant provided jobs as well as raising the standard of living for a lot of people in town. The place was full of no pressure no skills jobs. Work, just work.

Of the shanties making it through the winters one remained to be occupied regularly. The old man topped in his dirt and grease-rimmed beige cap, khaki work clothes with most of the buttons, and flat worn work boots, was the only survivor to spend more than two consecutive seasons in one of the shacks.

His was built of weathered unfinished plywood sheets, held up by plywood braces, screws, nails, and tarpaper. The recently acquired pot-belly stove was a real luxury. The walls spread for fifteen feet, stood eight feet high in front, sloping to a sufficient seven in the rear. Windows were non-existent. The door was strapped to the wall with leather hinges and a cloth lock. A chair and two apple boxes along with the stove decorated the floor. A cot stood against the back wall. A picture of the Sacred Heart of Jesus gripped one wall while the opposite wall carried a picture of the Blessed Virgin Mary. The blankets on the cot were never used by the dogs unless one of them was sick. A sick dog took over the rights to the cot as well as a blanket.

In many ways the old man resembled his abode. Both were weathered and gray. The old man had an untrimmed beard and white hair that rimmed the balding top of his head. The cap he wore kept what hair he had flat to his head while it shaded his eyes and the top of his nose. The nose which evenly separated his face had never been broken. It set straight between his shining brown wet eyes and dusky cheeks. His lips hid under his beard and mustache. The teeth he had were old man's teeth, worn, a bit too long, mostly straight, but chipped here and there. His dirt-washed, calloused-smooth hands, fit him well. He had no trouble standing as upright as he could in the little house.

After all the dogs were fed in the morning he retired to his house to say his prayers. When the whistle blew at six he made sure his fire was not too busy burning wood. He then set out hiking away across the railroad track to the farming area that stretched for miles on the west side of town. The month of June was cherry picking time. Unless he got a job thinning fruit he took a vacation during July till pear harvest in August. In the fall was apple harvest time. Winter was always reserved for pruning. All in all he did not have an over active work routine. After working his day he would start back to the shanty. Sometimes on his way he passed people who worked at the plant. They were going home to their families. He smiled and greeted them. Those who paid no attention to him he would see some other day.

When he got back to his shanty the coals in the stove were usually still good for starting a fire, so he would not have to use up a match. Heating up leftovers from the morning meal and his lunch made an evening meal to feed the dogs.

On Sundays when the workers didn't come to the plant he would go to the town. The Catholic Church he attended was near enough. Many of the workers went to mass there too. Some saw him, but paid less attention then to the bedraggled scraggly-bearded old man, who only took his hat off in church, than when they were walking home.

Many of the children in church watched him walk to communion. He smiled at all of them, receiving in return smiles and faces peeping from behind mother's skirts. After he received communion from the priest he would return to his private spot in the back of the church to sit alone. After church he usually went home to his place and went to bed; because, after all for him it was the Good Lord's day of rest too.

The next day being a Monday didn't make any difference to the dogs who scratched, while some even barked as they waited for him to appear. When he opened the door he was hatless, more stooped and drained looking. He fed them and received their love, but was unable to reciprocate. He stayed in most of the day.

Only once in all the time he lived there did he have a visitor. Who happened to come the Monday when he didn't feel well, hadn't been able to go work, to get food, or light a fire. The visitor from the plant said the corporation needed the land on which he was living. The old man would have to move. The old man nodded his understanding. The old man apologized for not being able to give his visitor anything. The fellow said he didn't have time anyway as he told the old man the plant was expanding, the town was growing.

While his visitor talked the old man thought that there would be more inquisitive children in church whose parents would continue listening to the whistle of the plant.

Tuesday morning the dogs came in the open door of the old man's house for breakfast. It was in a bowl close to the warm potbelly stove. The old man put it there the night before, fixing it prior to relighting a fire, saying his night prayers, then dying in his sleep.

The End

ABOUT THE AUTHOR

Since the age of thirteen, Richard Bustetter has worked an extraordinarily wide variety of jobs, giving him unique insight into the range of ways people live. These jobs have included janitor's helper, welder, paper boy, office employee, resident assistant at a college dorm, farm laborer, childcare worker, ranch hand, Trappist monk, Roman Catholic seminarian, tractor driver, registered nurse, and now author.

Richard Bustetter received a BA in English from the University of Portland. He currently lives in an old farmhouse near Yakima, Washington, with his wife of nearly twenty years.

m

M Lucey 1963

Janemarie63

M gleeson 63.

Mary gleeson 42 @gmail.com.

M gleeson 63.